I0781291

THE UNKNOWN AMONG US

NYXARA TORA

WORKBOOK PRESS LLC
187 E Warm Springs Rd,
Suite B285 Las Vegas NV 89119 USA

Website: https://workbookpress.com/
Hotline: 1-888-818-4856
Email: admin@workbookpress.com

Ordering Information:

Quantity sales. Special discounts are available on quantity purchases by corporations, associations, and others. For details, contact the publisher at the address above.

Library of Congress Control Number:

ISBN-13:   978-1-963718-55-3   Paperback Version
                  978-1-965732-10-6   Digital Version

REV. DATE: 12/05/2024

THE UNKNOWN AMONG US

by

NYXARA TORA

TRIGGER WARNINGS

This book may not be suitable for all readers. Triggers are listed below!

Emotional, physical, sexual abuse, torture, abusive relationship, abandonment, violence, death, depression, attempted crimes, bondage, adoption, child abuse, confinement, family conflict, forced actions, gaslighting, graphic death and sex, kidnapping, murder, nudity, panic attacks, physical assault, poverty, profanity, religious conflict, rape, stabbing, substance abuse, suicidal ideation, victim blaming, verbal abuse.

ACKNOWLEDGMENT

I would like to give my thanks and appreciation to all my friends and family who believed in me and spent many times listening to my rambles about the fun facts of my book.

I'd love to thank my special Moon for believing in me, keeping me on a strict timeline, and not letting me give up when I wanted to.

I want to give a special thank you to Vix, the amazing 'Stavros', who has helped me every step of the way with editing and writing the sexy bits. We spent many long nights together working on this. So much coffee was needed!

I love you all, thank you for being such amazing people!

☽ PROLOGUE ☾

The wind was cold and the rain was so loud against the shingles on the roof that it was the only thing to be heard at the dead of night, except for the crying. It seemed to be so loud that it blocked out the sound of the wind and rain. He stood there, his face covered by the hood of his long coat, listening to the crying inside the rundown cottage. The windows were all broken, the front door was broken down, not a single light around him.

Wolves howled in the distance, maybe it was time for him to leave? But the crying kept his attention and perhaps his life would have turned out differently if he did turn and walk away. Who knows, maybe his life would have been filled with riches if he had just left. It was a thought that had crossed his mind many times after this night, how much different his life would be if he had turned and left, but he couldn't go back in time to stop himself from walking into that broken down cottage.

The soggy ground squished under his boots as he walked towards the cottage, the moonlight offered little light between the stormy clouds. He paused for a moment by the wooden steps, listening for any sounds of life other than the crying but all he heard were the wolves howling in the distance.

The steps made a groan of discomfort as he walked up them, though he was sure that if his coat were any heavier from the rain, the wooden steps would have collapsed under the pressure of his boots. He wasn't sure what he was expecting when he walked inside, maybe a wild animal running around or a frightened parent jumping out at him with a weapon screaming at him to leave, but there was nothing.

He took in his surroundings, and as he did he was sure a wild animal had to have gotten in there from the amount of blood everywhere. It seemed to have covered the walls and floors, he could even see pieces of what he assumed to be human flesh and bones. He couldn't smell the blood or rotting flesh, though he wasn't sure if it was just the overpowering smell of rain masking the scent or if it was all just dried up. His eyes scanned around, trying to figure out what had actually happened there. Dishes were shattered, chairs and tables flipped over or broken, even pictures had some form of damage to them as if whatever or whoever attacked this place wanted to make sure every inch of the cottage was damaged.

The crying snapped him out of his thoughts and he began to walk once more while being careful not to disturb anything around him. He made his way through what looked to be the living room, or what was left of it, and walked into a hallway. He stopped once more, the crying was louder now, after taking a small breath he walked down the hallway and stopped at the ajar door. The crying stopped as he lifted his hand and pushed the door open with his finger. The door creaked in disagreement of having to move. It seemed odd to the male, as he stepped into the bedroom, that the room was barely touched, unlike the rest of the cottage.

Lightning flashed outside and the male's eyes moved over the room slowly until finally stopping on the source of the crying. The man crouched down slowly but remained silent for a moment as he watched the little movement coming from behind a chest of sorts. Maybe it was a chest of clothing? Or toys? He honestly didn't care about what was in the chest but he was curious to see who it was crying behind the chest. "Don't worry, I won't harm you," he spoke. His voice was rough and stern but also gentle. "Come with me. There's nothing left for you here." He slowly held out a hand.

The man discovered it was a small child, perhaps five or six, and it was a boy. The little child seemed unsure at first, maybe feeling safer in the darkness? Or maybe he was just frightened by what had happened in this cottage. The man remained patient and calm as the small boy worked up his courage to step around the chest and walk forward. The man could see the filth that covered the boy, blood and mud, most of his clothing was torn off or ripped bad enough that it was barely staying together, and the man could see some bruises and scratches.

Soon the boy stood in front of him and held up his arms to be lifted. The man arched his brow but then just smiled and wrapped his arms around the boy then wrapped him up in the coat as he was lifted. "You are safe now," he whispered. He turned and began to walk out of the cottage, trying to keep the shivering boy warm against his chest. The crying had stopped, it no longer bothered his ears as he walked away from the cottage and into the woods that surrounded them. The man looked down at the boy who stared up at him with fear but maybe also relief.

Such things were unclear to him. He lifted his eyes to look forward as he and the child vanished into the darkness of the night.

☽ CHAPTER ONE ☾

Ten Years Later

Two teens strolled down an abandoned road wearing dark clothing to blend into the night. "Your father is going to kill us. Dead. We are so dead and it's all your fault," A blond boy said,

glaring at his black shaggy haired best friend. He removed his glasses nervously to clear the fog before pushing them back up his nose.

"Relax. He won't kill us because he isn't going to find out," the dark haired teen said, laughing up at the taller boy.

The taller boy shivered as he clung to his jacket "Forgive me for not having the same faith as you, Ash, but that scary ass giant-of-a-father of yours finds out everything. You remember when we got caught trying to steal his car?"

"How can I forget? You remind me of it every other day, Liam." Ash rolled the sleeves of his shirt as he shook his head. "That happened like two years ago. Can't you let it go already?" He stopped in his tracks looking at Liam with a puzzled look "And I wasn't trying to steal it, I was just borrowing it." He said matter- of- factly as he proceeded to walk "We only got caught because, one, we tried stealing it out of the drive-"

"Aha! So you admit we tried stealing it," Liam jumped in before stumbled over a rock in the dirt road.

Ash rolled his eyes and continued "-Two, because you suck at being a look out and didn't tell me he was watching us from the door and Three, get new glasses cause you can't see."

"It's not my fault his face screams 'Death to all the maggots that walk this earth.'" He recovered his steps "I swear you should hunt down your real parents. Maybe they're rich! Or maybe they look less scary. Either way it would be a good idea t-"

Ash blocked him out at this point. Liam always rambled about this when they were doing something that might be considered stupid. Ash had found out he was adopted five years ago when he had snooped through his father's office and found the paperwork about it. He didn't ask questions about it and he honestly never cared what the reasons were for why he was put up for adoption. As far as he saw it, Stavros was his father and loved him and took great care of him, so why would he complain about that? He was picked to be his son, unlike Liam who was stuck with his abusive drunk father and distant mother who seemed to want nothing to do with Liam anyways.

The excitement started creeping up on Ash because they were headed to an old abandoned asylum, rumored to be haunted. It had been condemned when Ash was around ten, his father said some of the people who lived there went insane one night and killed over twenty people, some who worked there and some who lived there, and then tried burning the place down.

Luckily the cops had been called along with the firefighters and EMTs so the fire was put out quickly enough. It was supposed to be torn down but someone decided to buy the land. They must have lost funding or something because nothing ever happened with the place and it still stood there with a large fence around it.

"Shh. We're here." Ash said, cutting Liam off his ramble.

They looked up at the building and on the outside it actually looked normal, mostly. The building was six stories high and made of what seemed to have been white brick. The windows all looked like they had been broken and scorched from the fire that surrounded some of them on the third floor, but other than that it looked fine.

"Can't we just go get lucky with some chicks?" Liam whispered. Yeah he didn't like doing all these dumb things that would land him in trouble.

"Chicks?" Ash smirked. "When have you ever called them 'chicks?' And when have you ever had an interest in them?"

Liam shrugged "I'm allowed to like girls too. Who says I can't like both?"

"I thought being gay kinda meant you didn't like girls?" Ash asked, raising a brow. "I'm not gay. I'm bisexual. So I am allowed to like both," Liam muttered.

Ash chuckled and shook his head "Whatever you say." looking back at the fence that stood between them and the building "Anyways, no, we can't leave. We're here now. If you wanted to do something else you should have spoken up sooner."

"I did!" Liam exclaimed.

"Well clearly I wasn't listening." Ash smirked. "That, or, your idea was stupidly boring. Now stop being a scaredy cat and hurry up before someone sees us." Ash held back a laugh hearing Liam grumbled under his breath, "You need hearing aids."

Liam struggled his way through the gap in the fence, probably cut because some other kids decided to break in a while ago, and waited for Ash on the other side.

Ash slipped in behind him and looked around slowly while listening to make sure no one was around them.

"Well we haven't been killed, yet, so let's go inside" Ash grinned, heading towards the red front door.

"Inside? You want to go inside? Why? What if other people are in there and they decide to torture us or kills us or even eat us!" Liam's voice was filled with panic and fear, Ash found it amusing in all honesty.

"I'll just have to outrun you so they'll catch you and I can get away." Ash chuckled menacingly. "Haha. You are so not funny." Liam rolled his eyes as he spoke.

"I am hilarious." Ash said with a grin. He nudged Liam and then headed up the stone steps. Liam looked around as he followed beside Ash and really hated how he could look so unbothered while he was almost trembling in fear. He didn't like the idea of trying to see ghosts even if that was why they were there, it wasn't a happy thought for him, it was a terrifying one. People liked to carry on about how they saw ghosts in this building or heard them and so Ash came up with the brilliant idea to go see if it was true. It was great being his best friend at times, but this wasn't one of those times.

The front doors were ajar, leaning on chains that were bolted into the brick and mortar, honestly the only thing keeping them standing somewhat upright. Ash squeezed through the crack first, followed by Liam. They both looked around, greeted by a long hallway with six doors on each side, eerily ajar. There was a lobby with a sitting area to their right but it had been trashed like a tornado gone through leaving paper and chairs thrown about. What looked to be blood was on the walls and floors, though it looked old, or at least Liam hoped it was old. The only light shining in the place was from a street light but it didn't really show a whole lot around them, only being able to make out shapes but not really much detail. Ash had taken out his cell phone and turned on the flashlight so they could see around better. He noticed some spray paint on the walls, graffiti from wanna be taggers and gang members everywhere with some writing along the lines of 'Death to those who enter', 'They see you', or 'Suck my dick.'

Ash already knew anything worth any kind of money would have been looted by now, not that he really cared. He wasn't here to steal stuff, he was here to try seeing if the rumors about ghosts living here were true. So far no luck.

"Okay so we went inside. Can we go now?" Liam whispered as if hiding from the ghosts.

Ash ignored Liam and started to walk down the hallway sighing when he heard Liam trip over something and curse but didn't bother turning to look.

"I think I hear cops coming. Can we leave? What if they think we are Satan worshipers and shoot us?" Liam whispered.

Ash rolled his eyes and shook his head slowly "The cops aren't coming and they wouldn't shoot us for worshiping the devil. Stop whining," he murmured. He heard Liam grumbling to himself and chuckled softly. "I find myself with a massive headache every time we hang out."

"And I find a new religion every time we hang out. Why you think it's a great idea to do these stupid things is beyond me. It's like being convinced that knocking on the devil's door and running away is a great idea."

"I highly doubt the devil lives here and if he does we really should tell him to hire a decorator." Ash joked.

"Yeah, let's do that, because I'm sure the devil would be so thrilled to stand here and listen to your scrawny ass bitch about how unclean his home is," Liam said sarcastically. He had no idea how he let Ash convince him every time to do dumb shit like this, it always landed them in trouble, and he had an uneasy feeling this might just be one of those times. After all, who in their right mind thought hunting ghosts was fun.

Ash chuckled softly to himself and looked around, thoughts of exploring the rooms did seem tempting but he already knew there wasn't anything really worth looking at. Besides, he wanted to explore the top floors and what better help than the new ghost hunting app he had found.

Looking back down at his phone he opened the app watching as a line circled around what seemed to be a green radar map.

Liam, realizing he had fallen too far behind Ash, briskly walked to catch up beside Ash just to see his phone in hand with that stupid ghost app up.

"Do you really believe that dumb app actually works?" Liam scoffed.

Ash rolled his eyes, "Of course it works." just as a blip appeared on the radar in front of them. Ash perked up excitedly, "See! I told you!" he said cheerfully, while making his way to the nearest room that the blip was in.

Liam about jumped out of his skin hearing the blip echo in the hallway. "Ash, I'm too young and sexy to die, let's not and say we did." He tried to convince Ash, who clearly did not have the brain cell today.

Ash paused outside the door, leaning his head over enough to peek within the room. While doing so, he saw a shadow move from one side of the room to the other, crossing in front of the windows.

'BEHIND YOU' the app said in a masculine robotic voice.

Ash jumped back almost losing his footing "Did you see that?" he whispered. Liam froze mid step "Fuck seeing, did you hear what that said!"

'RUN' the app said once more

Ash shifts his eyes to look at his best friend, too scared to move only to see a large shadow standing at the beginning of the hallway. His bright blue eyes widened with fear as all the color drained from his face.

"What?" Liam exclaimed, a small tremor in his voice as the hair on his neck started to stand. *'TROUBLE'* the app pings as a blip shows up exactly where the shadow stood.

"Don't play this game with me, you made the app do that! You had to, right!?" he frantically hissed out.

Ash looked forward intently staring at the door before him too scared to move or look at the ghost that stood between them and their only exit "Don't turn around… it looks lik-"

"Two boys in serious trouble?" A deep voice boomed behind them.

From the outside of the building two screams of young teenage boys can be heard along with the caws of crows flying away.

☽ CHAPTER TWO ☾

Both boys stood hugging each other for dear life, their eyes clamped shut as Liam cried and Ash looked whiter than paper.

The supposed shadow stood taller than the doorway, blocking out most of the light besides what haloed around him. A sigh escaped the shadows mouth making Ash slowly open his eyes, he knew that sigh, having heard it many times within his life. Slowly he turned his eyes to the side "Dad?" Ash croaked out

"What are you guys doing in here?" Stavros growled out. Oh yeah, he was pissed.

Liam unswallowed his heart, not sure if he was relieved or not that it was Ash's father "So much for him not finding out," he hissed under his breath.

"We… um…" Ash couldn't think of a lie. Not that lying was even a good idea since his dad always seemed to tell when Ash lied. "We wanted to check it out."

Stavros crossed his arms over his chest "You wanted to check out the asylum?" He asked. His voice was deep with anger. "You thought it was okay to come look inside? You didn't think that the fence outside was a way to keep people out? Or even the 'keep out' signs that are posted everywhere?"

Ash opened his mouth to speak but ended up just shutting it. He knew nothing he said right now would make this better.

"Let's go," Stavros growled out. He didn't move till Liam and Ash slipped past him with their heads down. He remained silent as he gave one good look towards the door the boys were at, watching for a brief moment. Scowling he turned to follow behind the boys outside, past the fence, to a black Jaguar parked on the side of the road. He slipped into the driver's seat while both boys slipped into the back.

Stavros started the car and took off driving. He wasn't going to bring Liam to his father's house, he knew the man was probably drunk right now anyways and he didn't want Liam getting beaten for doing a stupid teenager thing. The boys didn't utter a word as Stavros drove silently towards Liam's mothers. He stopped in front of an ugly soft pink house and felt like cringing. How could anyone have a pink house? Gross. He got out of the car and walked onto the sidewalk, he only stopped to look back to make sure Liam was actually following him, before he pushed the small white gate open, and waited for Liam to walk ahead of him. He followed two steps behind him and walked inside once Liam had unlocked and opened the front door.

"Good evening, Lucy." Stavros greeted, stepping inside behind Liam.

Lucy, a thin woman, had been heading down the stairs hearing the front door opening. "Stavros" She greeted softly. She tucked a loose strand of blonde hair behind her ear once she got to the bottom of the stairs.

"Liam, where have you been? I've been worried sick!" Lucy moved over to Liam to look him over as she spoke. Once she inspected him to make sure he had no wounds, she pulled him into a hug while lightly smacking him on the back of the head. "You can't just leave without saying anything, Liam. You'll give me a heart attack doing that."

Stavros watched the two with a faint smile seeing how Liam towered over the tiny lady. Lucy was a very small woman, at least compared to Stavros, standing ruffly below his chest and weighed 100 pounds soaking wet.

"I'm sorry, mom," Liam murmured softly. He hugged her back and shut his eyes for a moment, knowing he'd better enjoy this moment before Stavros ruined it.

Stavros softly cleared his throat, "I can't stay long but earlier when you called me I saw that Ash was also missing, figured they would be together." he explained.

"Thank you, Stavros," Lucy said with a soft smile. "I'm going to have to tie a bell around his neck so I can hear when he tries leaving." she teased with a soft laugh.

Stavros was starting to think he'd have to do that with Ash too in order to keep the boy from doing something stupid; like breaking into an asylum to hunt for ghosts.

Stavros gave a soft chuckle back as his gaze went to Liam, who had stepped back from his mom's embrace. "I caught them in that abandoned asylum." Stavros spoke up, knowing Liam wouldn't.

Lucy gasped, narrowing her eyes at Liam, "You have been told not to go there. It's dangerous! They have a fence around it for a reason, Liam, what were you thinking?" she demanded. "Well-I- Ash- we-" Liam stumbled over his words. "Clearly we weren't thinking," he confidently said.

Lucy smacked him on the arm, "Clearly not, young man!" She snapped, smacking him on the arm a few more times.

Stavros may not get along with Lucy all that much but he did admire her strength. She may be tiny but after putting up with abuse from Liam's father she sure did learn how to fight and could do serious damage with a single punch.

"You are grounded. Go eat your dinner, which is now cold, and then do those dishes before going straight to your room!. No tv, computer, or phone, or.. Or hanging out with Ash for a good week! You be thankful I'm not telling your father about this."

"My school work is on my computer" Liam murmured softly.

Lucy huffed as she crossed her arms, "Fine. You can use it just for school and nothing else. Now get going." she said firmly.

Liam opened his mouth to speak but with a heavy sigh, he kept his head low while removing his shoes and headed to the kitchen.

Stavros stepped back towards the door, ready to bid them goodnight but paused, "You won't be telling his father, correct?" he asked once Liam was out of ear shot.

"Of course not, why would I do something so stupid like that?" Lucy spat at him. Her hands went to her hips as she narrowed her eyes on Stavros.

With a soft sigh, he shook his head, "You really shouldn't use his father as a threat." he said. Normally he wouldn't really pry into another family's life however Dan, Liam's father, was an abusive drunk and it was easy to see the fear in the boy anytime the man was brought up. "How about you mind your own business and keep Ash on a tight leash so he doesn't keep getting Liam into trouble." she snapped at him. "Liam doesn't normally cause any trouble until he is around your boy so I'll parent my child however I wish and you parent yours. Now get out." Stavros actually rolled his eyes at that but held his tongue. He had so many things he could say but he had his own child to punish and he knew arguing with stupid was very pointless. "Goodnight." Stavros finally said. Yeah, he didn't get along with Liam's parents. One was a drunk that Stavros wanted to punch everytime he saw him, and the other was just thick headed.

Ash felt like shit that Liam was in trouble and he just hoped Dan didn't find out about this. His father was inside for about five minutes before he left the house and returned to the car. He started it up once again and drove home in silence. Ash thought about what to say but he knew there was nothing he really could say to explain why he did something stupid like this. This wasn't the worst thing he has ever done, so at least that was a plus. Right?

They got home far too quickly for Ash's liking. His dad pulled into the driveway and shut the car off. Stavros got out first, shutting the door a bit harder than he normally did. Ash took in a deep breath, exhaling slowly while exiting the car and dragging his feet as he headed inside. The house had two floors as well as a basement. The outside was always kept clean because his father had hired a groundskeeper. It didn't look like they really needed one because the yard wasn't all that big in the front but the backyard was big enough to have a pond, pool, and a garden. Ash never bothered to really think about how big the property was but now that he thought about it, it was pretty big and happily they didn't have neighbors right beside them either.

Ash dreaded going inside because he knew his father was upset with him but he didn't really have much of a choice. He removed his shoes once they got inside and put them away while his dad removed his own shoes and coat.

"Dad… I'm really sorry..." Ash said softly.

Stavros glared down at him. "Sorry," he echoed. "Ash…" He sighed and rubbed his temples. "What were you thinking?" He tossed his keys and wallet onto the console table. "Why did you think it was a good idea to go there? You know what could have happened, right?" He stopped, turning to Ash with a scowl "A lot of homeless people go in there, druggies go in there. What would you have done if they were there? What if the cops showed up?" he asked seriously.

Ash rubbed the back of his neck, "I wasn't thinking about that..."

"Clearly." Stavros growled out. "You guys could have gotten hurt in there. That isn't a place for you or Liam to be hanging out and you're lucky I got there before one of you got seriously hurt." "How did you find us?" Ash asked nervously. It wasn't like Ash left a note or anything.

"Besides the unpleasant call from Lucy, I activated the GPS on your cell." Stavros said, as he walked to the left into the living room and sat down on the couch with a sigh. The kitchen was beside the living room and had a door leading to the backyard . His dad's office was to the right by the front door but it was always locked and Ash wasn't allowed in there. Stairs leading up to the second floor were between his dads office and the game room.

"Why?" Ash asked with a frown, stopping at the living room archway.

Stavros raised a brow as he looked at him. "Why?" he repeated, tilting his head in disbelief, "After you and Liam decided to stay out all night without saying anything and worrying not only me, but Lucy as well, I had decided that GPS needs to remain on."

That hadn't been a good time, Ash and Liam had decided to get drunk and ended up hanging around the creek all night. It was a fun night but it was not fun once he got home. He had never seen his father get that angry before and he never wanted to see that look again, it was like looking death in the face.

"Are you trying to worry me to death?" Stavros asked, his brows folded downwards. "Because you are doing a great job at it. I know, you are a teenager, but damn it Ash you don't need to be causing some kind of trouble every other week. There is plenty for you and Liam to do that doesn't involve pissing me off or getting yourselves killed."

Ash heard this so many times. He knew his dad was right but he thought by now his father would have a different lecture to give or something. He heard his father speaking again and made the mistake of not really paying attention because the look his father was currently giving him wasn't a pleasant one.

"Well?" Stavros growled out.

"What?" Ash asked before shrugging slightly "I… Don't know what you asked," he admitted. Stavros stood quickly. "Go to your room. Right now!" He snapped, pointing to the stairs.

Ash quickly obeyed and ran upstairs to avoid angering his dad even more.

Stravos ran his fingers through his hair in frustration, pacing around the living room, not knowing what to do with his sons' behavior. Those thoughts, though, came to an abrupt end as his cellphone rang making him curse under his breath "who the fuck?" seeing the number come across his screen he answered but said nothing as the voice started to speak right away.

Standing still within the room a dark laughter escaped his lips, this really wasn't the fucking day. "Are you serious?" Stavros snarled, clearly not in the mood for this. He narrowed his eyes at the wall as he listened and debated on whether or not he seriously needed this phone. He walked to his office and stepped inside once he unlocked it. His office was full of shelves that had a lot of books on it, some looked really old and worn out while others looked like they hadn't been touched. He had a large brown desk with a laptop on it, some papers, and pens. He didn't bother turning on the ceiling light, he just turned the small desk light on and sat down on the desk chair.

He rubbed his face as he sighed for what felt like the 20th time today. "I really don't have time for this right now. Stop by tomorrow at noon." He hung up before the person could respond. He groaned as he sat back in his chair and shut his eyes to think.

Ash had changed into some pj bottoms and was sitting on his bed. His room was covered in band posters, with a small simple desk in the corner for his laptop and a dresser beside it. The door to his closet was at the end of his bed.

He had been texting Liam for a few minutes but he assumed Liam's mom took his cell away because Liam stopped talking. Ash had no idea how long it would be before his dad took away his cell. He idly looked at his phone and saw it was 11:30 PM now and he knew he should be sleeping but he couldn't. He finally heard his dad heading upstairs and thought he'd come to his room but heard his dad's bedroom door shut. Great, now he had to wait until tomorrow to finish talking about this.

Ash sighed, "Fuck..." he muttered to himself as he thought about how stupid he could be at times. He put his cell on the nightstand and then laid down under the blanket to get some sleep.

☽ CHAPTER THREE ☾

Ash rolled out of bed the next morning and groaned as he stretched. He glanced around his room for a moment before walking over to his dresser, pulling out some clothes to dress. He grabbed his cell from the nightstand, checked it to see if he had any messages, then slipped it into his pocket when he saw none. Ash let out a slow breath as he opened his door and was instantly greeted by the smell of coffee. He cringed just slightly knowing his father was awake, not that he was really surprised since it was 8am and his dad seemed to be up with the sunrise. Shoving the thought of just returning to bed to avoid his dad out of his mind, Ash headed down the stairs and into the kitchen.

"Good morning," Ash hesitantly said, trying to gauge his dad's mood.

Stavros, who was reading the paper while sipping his coffee, didn't even glance at Ash when he entered the kitchen. "Morning." he replied in a short tone.

Ash almost actually whimpered at that, knowing just by that response his father was still pretty peeved at him. Ash opened a cupboard to grab a bowl, then scurried silently around the kitchen for the rest of the items. Once he got his bowl filled with cereal he sat at the other end of the table furthest from his dad and stared at the table while he ate, wishing he was invisible.

"So." Stavros started, setting his cup of coffee on the table alongside the paper he had been reading to lean back in his chair, his gaze seeming to burn a hole through Ash.

Ash's hand holding the spoon paused halfway to his mouth as his eyes slowly moved up to look at his dad, "Yes?"

There were times Stavros really felt like strangling Ash, this was starting to be one of those times. "Anything to say for yourself?" he asked, a bit impatiently.

"No," Ash said, way before he could stop himself. He knew he needed to work harder on thinking before speaking. Sure, he really didn't have anything to say for himself but didn't mean he could get away with saying nothing!

"No?" Stavros almost growled out.

Oh yeah, Ash knew that tone of voice. He fucked up.

"Okay, how about 'I'm sorry, dad, for making you and Liam's mother worry so badly. I'm sorry for making you have to hunt us down while thinking the worst things had happened.'" Stavros' tone was sharp and he was losing patients fast.

Ash swallowed hard and shifted uncomfortably in his chair, "I am sorry.." he said in a soft voice. He already apologized, didn't he? He was pretty sure he did.

"Sorry for making me worry so much or sorry because you got caught?"

Ash looked away and remained silent for a moment too long because he heard the heavy sigh leave his father.

"Damnit, Ashton. Do you have any idea what could have happened? You know that area is unsafe. They didn't put a fence there just for decoration. You or Liam could have got seriously hurt"

"Well, Liam did trip once or twice." Ash almost laughed under his breath.

Stavros' eyes widened, giving that all-too-famous, dad look that made Ash sink further into his seat whispering "Sorry."

Stavros let out yet another sigh, "You could have run into drug dealers there or gang members or been killed. I had hoped, after the whole shit show of stealing my car, you would have at least started to think before you act." Stavros' tone softened just slightly. He was used to giving this kind of lecture to his son by now but he had really hoped it'd be a long while before he needed to do it again.

Ash set his spoon down in his bowl and wrapped his arms around himself as he tried thinking of what to say. It wasn't his fault they lived in such a small, boring, town with nothing fun to do.

Ash went to speak, but before he could even open his mouth, Stavros cut him off.

"What's worse is you could have gotten Liam in serious trouble. You know how his father would have reacted to this, did you even stop to think about that?" his father asked.

Ash hated how bad he felt but he knew his dad was right. Liam hadn't even wanted to go to begin with but, like always, Ash dragged him along with his stupid plan.

"I can do better." Ash finally whispered, not daring to look back at his father.

Stavros remained silent as he stood and poured himself another cup of coffee hoping the second cup would prevent a murder.

"All I ask is that you try. You aren't a bad kid, Ash, but you really need to think before you act. I don't want the cops knocking on my door one night to let me know you are seriously injured in the hospital from doing something stupid, or worse, killed." Stavros said. Who knew raising a teenager was so damn hard. Once he refilled his cup, he turned to look at Ash, his face grim with disappointment.

"You are grounded for a week. Leave your phone on the table, finish your breakfast, and then head up to your room. I want you to bring me your laptop, grab a pen and paper from the coffee table and write a five page essay on why what you did was wrong and once that is finished bring it to me." Stavros' tone left no room for argument as he sat back in his chair.

Ash just gave a small nod, finishing his breakfast quickly, he placed his cell on the table once he stood up. He washed his dishes and started to leave when his dad spoke again.

"Ash." Stavros began, his gaze cutting into the boy. "Don't make me start to question if I'm being too lenient on you because I'll tell you now, it doesn't matter if you are nine, sixteen or even sixty years old, I'll still yank you over my knee and spank your bare ass."

Paling at those words, Ash just gave a quick nod of understanding and wasted no time in running up to his room. He swore his ass twitched in phantom pain from past spankings he's received and he did not need, nor want, a reminder of the actual pain of one.

It was almost noon when a loud knock sounded on the front door. Stavros didn't even need to answer to know who it was. With an irritated sigh, he got up from his desk chair and went to the front door. He paused, taking a few seconds to calm the already rising anger, before he opened the door. He stared at the two men for a moment and without a word, he stepped to the side and gestured for them to enter.

"Hello, Stavros." One man said, stepping inside. "Greetings," the second man followed behind the first.

Both males were about two inches shorter than him and are actually brothers who Stavros hadn't seen in quite a few years and, sadly, that wasn't nearly long enough.

Stavros just gave a nod of his head to them while he shut the door and led them both to his office so they could speak in private.

"What do you two want?" Stavros almost growled after he shut his door and walked to his chair. He took a seat and crossed his arms as he looked at the two, wanting a portal to appear below them and swallow them up; however he pushed that thought aside. He could be.. Civil, for the moment.

"I told you he wasn't listening." the male with black hair and a goatee said with an amused voice.

"Shut up, Patrick." Tyler, who had short brown hair, snapped. He took a seat across the desk from Stavros and cleared his throat, "We-"

"We are sight seeing," Patrick cut in, sitting on the other chair beside Tyler, "What do you think we want?" His voice dripped of sarcasm, he was highly amused at how annoyed Stavros got whenever they were around.

Stavros pinched the bridge of his nose as his eyes shut and muttered under his breath, "Killing is a crime," about a dozen times. Why did he tell them to stop by?.

Tyler gave Patrick a glare, really wishing he would just shut up for once so his mouth didn't get them in trouble. "We are hoping to settle here for a few months," He started, turning his gaze back over to Stavros. "If that is okay, and, if so, where do you recommend we eat?"

Stavros already knew that's why they were here, of course, but it's still polite to ask. He stayed silent for a minute or two as he thought over a few things. He supposed it wouldn't be the worst thing in the world and besides, he did have errands to attend to and having the extra help would make it go faster.

"There is a motel in the east end, it's not the best in town but it is closer to the best restaurants so I say stay there and eat your fill." Stavros said, a small, knowing, smirk forming on his lips. "I do require your help with something, Tyler." he continued, "It won't be for a few days so take that time to get settled and browse around " he suggested.

Tyler and Patrick looked pleased with Stavros' words, until the last part.

"My help?" Tyler questioned, but gave a quick nod of his head seeing Stavros raise his brow, "Yeah, of course, anything you need."

"You don't need my help?" Patrick asked, already planning to have a few ladies over while Tyler was gone.

Stavros slowly rose to his feet, clearly signaling the end of their meeting, "I do, actually, but I'll fill you both in on the details at a later time. Keep in touch and let me know how things are going." he said, walking to his office door and paused to turn back to them, who had also stood and were following behind him.

"Keep a sharp eye on the shadows, you never know what could be lurking in them." Stavros warned. He opened his office door and blinked seeing Ash standing on the other side, hand raised up, ready to knock.

"Why are you out of your room?" Stavros asked, a bit more stern than he meant to.

Ash slowly lowered his hand to his side and gave a quick glance behind his father, curious about the two males who stood behind him. He felt the hairs on the back of his neck stand up but he didn't understand why, maybe because he never met them before? Maybe because he's never seen random people coming out of his fathers office? It did make him wonder why the three were in his fathers soundproof office, he's never seen his father bring home any woman before… it actually answered a few questions. Pushing all of those gross thoughts out of his head, he turned his attention back to his father.

"I finished the essay. I wasn't sure if I should leave it on the table or give it to you.." he trailed off with a light shrug.

"Good, I'll take it." Stavros said more gently. He took the papers from Ash once the boy held them up and gave them a quick glance but didn't get into reading the essay just yet. He decided it was best to see his guests off first and then he could settle down to read.

"Who are they?" Ash asked softly, glancing behind him again.

Stavros shook his head, "You can meet them when they come over for dinner in a few days. Now you go back to your room." he said firmly. He honestly didn't want to deal with introducing them now and plus, he knew with Patrick's smart mouth, it wouldn't be a quick introduction either.

Ash wanted to argue but he knew pushing his luck was not a smart idea especially after this morning. He looked at them one last time before he headed up to his room. He didn't understand the feeling in the pit of his stomach, a feeling of something very off, dread? Fear? He wasn't sure but it made him uneasy.

Stavros took the few steps to the front door, once Ash went upstairs, and opened it. "Come by for dinner tomorrow." Stavros said.

Patrick was curious about the boy who showed up and had many questions about it; however, the elbow to his gut from his brother kept him silent. He said nothing as he walked outside and paused long enough to wait for Tyler.

"See you tomorrow." Tyler confirmed. He stopped outside beside Patrick, "You better be on your best behavior." he hissed to his brother, and then began walking away from the house.

"You better get that stick removed from your ass" Patrick muttered under his breath, and followed after him.

☽ CHAPTER FOUR ☾

Ash poked at his eggs as he sat at the table and yawned. It had been uneventful the last two days and it sucked because he couldn't even find freedom in school since his fun adventure happened on Friday night and it was only Sunday. Only Sunday, he never thought he'd be so annoyed about the weekend going by so slowly. He knew Liam was grounded too and was still at his moms house, which did make him happy, at least he was out of his fathers reach for now. Sure, Lucy wasn't happy either but at least she wasn't going to let Liam's father find out. Ash forced himself to eat some of his breakfast but ended up throwing the rest out and washed the dishes. He had heard those guys arrive earlier this morning, but didn't have a chance to see them again. He was still curious on who they were and why they were here but more than that, he was curious on why he had that same feeling in the pit of his stomach, this time without even having to see them but just knowing they were here seemed to strike his every nerve.

Ash didn't stay downstairs long enough to talk though, he didn't want to see them because something about them felt wrong. He went upstairs to his room quickly and flopped down on his bed to work on calming his nerves. His mind began to daydream of Helliana, which wouldn't be the first time. She was this gorgeous fiery redhead at his school, he was smitten the moment he saw her. Her steel eyes looked like they could suck the soul out of anyone. Her hair, shit, he was sure it was softer than feathers. Ash hadn't spoken to her much but he was slowly working up to it, but it wasn't easy. She was an angel, her pale skin looked smoother than marble and that body of hers… Ash shook his head quickly to clear his thoughts, knowing if he kept thinking about that perfectly formed body of hers, he'd have a hard problem to handle.

He wasn't sure how much time had passed before he heard the front door close and then his father moving around downstairs. Since he was bored, and assumed his dad had a few chores for him to do, he decided to go downstairs.

"So.. Now can you tell me who those guys were?" Ash asked once he got to the kitchen. Stavros poured himself a cup of coffee as he spoke, "Tyler and Patrick. We used to work with each other a few years back."

"Yeah?" Ash tilted his head. "Wait, I thought you worked in your office?" He couldn't really remember a time when Stavros left the house for work.

Stavros gave a low chuckle, "I do work here, however at least twice a week I have to go into the office for meetings and other things. You are at school when I go in." he clarified, leaning against the counter to face Ash and sipped his coffee.

Ash silently thought that over but, since he didn't know everything his father did while he was away at school, he didn't dwell too hard.

"Why did you talk to them in your office?" Ash heard himself say, his mouth working faster than his brain.Stavros was a bit taken aback by that question but, assuming he was merely curious, he answered with a shrug, "Just seems easier than talking in here or the living room since all my work stuff is in my office."

Ash supposed that made sense, he remembered when he was younger he used to spend hours imagining what his father did in there. He came up with crazy ideas like his dad battled dragons or had a door to another world and so on but as he got older he realized that probably wasn't true. He did boring work all day long in there, not nearly as exciting as battling dragons but at least Ash wasn't left wondering anymore.

"So why are you down here, son?" Stavros broke the increasing silence.

Ash rapidly blinked, having gotten so lost in his head he forgot briefly why he even came downstairs.

"Oh, I was just curious on if I should start on any chores or something." Ash said enthusiastically while snapping his fingers.

"Ahh, so you're bored." Stavros had a hint of amusement in his voice.

"Bored? Why would I be bored?" Ash asked innocently. "I could be upstairs sleeping or counting my ceiling tiles." Ash continued, "Again." a small sigh escaped him.

Stavros snorted softly, "I'm not sure if you know this or not but being grounded isn't supposed to be fun. Weirdly enough, it's supposed to be boring and give you time to think about why you are being punished."

"I had the joys of writing a five page essay on that exact thing so I believe I've had plenty of time to think on that." Ash reminded him.

Stavros raised a brow at the boy, "Oh, well, " he started, pausing to take a sip of his coffee, "If it was such a joy I can always get you to write another essay on being a smart ass." he finished once he swallowed his sip.

"No!" Ash almost screamed with wide eyes. He cleared his throat and calmed himself, "I mean, no thank you." He lost this battle and he knew it but then again, he lost basically all of them.

Stavros crossed his arms over his chest and studied the boy for a moment. He knew Ash was bored, he always got restless having to lay around in his room all day with nothing to do which was why grounding was a perfect punishment, but it also meant Ash got a bit annoying always leaving his room.

"Tell you what. You remain in your room for the next three hours while I finish some work and then you can come down to sweep and mop the floors before Tyler and Patrick come over." Stavros offered.

Ash couldn't believe he was actually excited to do some stupid chore just to get out of his room but he'd take it. Whoever invented grounding as a punishment needed to be stabbed or something. Without another word, he spun around and quickly headed upstairs. He figured he could take a nap but that could wait until after he spent a little more time daydreaming of Helliana.

Later that day, not too long after Ash finished mopping the floors, Stavros went to the front door hearing a knock on it. He opened the door and tilted his head, "Have you gotten settled in and enjoying your time here?" he asked curiously.

Tyler stepped inside while chuckling lowly, "We haven't had a chance to try the restaurants but we saw a few promising spots.." He removed his jacket and hung it up on a hook by the door while stepping out of his shoes.

Patrick kicked off his shoes and made a face seeing the boy standing in the living room, "That's still here?" his voice had a hint of disgust in it.

Stavros glared at Pat, "*That* lives here." He said, a warning in his tone. "Permanently?" Patrick asked, shocked.

"What's for dinner? It smells amazing." Tyler cut in quickly, shooting a glare at Patrick. Patrick held his hands up in surrender and remained silent.

Ash felt that familiar feeling creep up on him again, every hair on the back of his neck stood up when Patrick had first looked at him. Something about these men wasn't right and he knew it, he just didn't know why but more than that, hearing a strong thick accent he couldn't place but as fast as that thought came it was replaced with shock "Excuse me? Did you just refer to me as 'That'?"

A slow smirk formed on Patrick's lips but he held his tongue since he felt the glare coming from Stavros.

Stavros walked past him towards Ash and gestured for everyone to get into the kitchen, "How about we just sit and eat." Why did he think this was a good idea? Patrick and Ash together in a room? Yeah, all his hair was going to be gray before the night ends.

"Ash, this is Patrick and Tyler. Guys, this is my son, Ash," Stavros said, pointing at each guy as he said their names. He took his seat and prayed for the patients he'd need to not kill everyone. "Nice meeting you, Ash," Tyler said, with a deep voice. Taking a seat, "This looks good, thank you for inviting us." he offered a smile.

"Hi," Patrick said uninterested. Why would he care about what that kid's name was?.

Ash just smiled and looked down at his plate having a hard time with the feeling of anxiousness in the pit of his stomach. His dad had made roast with mashed potatoes, caesar salad, and gravy.

Ash raised a brow a little as he watched Patrick struggle with eating. It was… interesting. The guy didn't seem to know how to properly hold a fork, let alone use it.

Ash swallowed a laugh watching this grown ass man struggle with a fork and looked to Tyler, "Does *that*" he pointed at Patrick, "Need my help?" he asked, slowly tilting his head. He elegantly lifted his fork to his mouth and took his mouthful.

Patrick glared daggers at the little shit as Tyler continued to help him with his struggles. He opened his mouth to snap at the shithead but before a word came out, Tyler quickly shoved food into his mouth to keep him quiet.

Ash slowly licked his lips and tauntingly held his fork, "Hey Patty, ever play 'here comes the airplane'?"

Stavros exhaled sharply seeing his prayers hadn't been answered as every patient he had went flying right out the window. "Behave, Ash, or else my belt will come flying off so fast it'll break the sound barrier."

Patrick laughed at Ash's pale face, "Yes, Ass, behave."

"Shut your mouth, Patty, or I'll use this belt on you too" Stavros snapped. He was ready to jump across this table and strangle them both.

"Stav, you can't do kinky play in front of the baby." Patrick said with a low gasp in fake horror at the thought.

"Anyway," Tyler quickly jumped in, hoping to change the topic. "Just eat the fucking roast Patrick and shut up." he hissed through his teeth.

"Me? What about *'that'*? I didn't do anything!" Patrick said in a defensive voice. "*That*' can at least eat with a fork." Ash retorted.

Stavros shoved away from the table as he shot to his feet, "ENOUGH!" he shouted. "I hear one more fucking word from either of you and I'll remove all the skin and muscle from your ass'." The pissed off look on his fathers face was enough to send a shiver down all their spines and make it well known death was coming to the next one who even breathed wrong. Once he was satisfied, Stavros returned to sitting resting his head in his hands to calm himself all over again and do some more praying for the much needed patients.

It got really awkward, just sitting there in silence while they ate, Ash clearly afraid to even sneeze. He couldn't finish his plate fast enough, glad when he could finally stand and took care of his dishes. He was about to pretty much run upstairs to his room however he froze when his father spoke.

"Oh Ash, before you leave." Stavros wiped his mouth with a napkin and leaned back in his chair. "Tyler and I are going to be leaving early tomorrow for business meetings. It's supposed to be a two day event but it might turn into three."

Ash nearly cheered at his fathers words, "Should I pack my bag tonight?" he asked, assuming he'd go to Liam's.

A grin grew on his fathers face and it was one Ash didn't like, "No, you both are grounded, remember? Besides, it's just Tyler and myself going so that leaves.-" he trailed off as his eyes drifted towards Patrick.

Ash was confused at first however his eyes began to grow wider and wider the more he listened. He followed his fathers eyes to Patrick and actually let out a laugh filled with disbelief, "No way, you're joking right? Doing a really late April fools prank?" There was no way his father was serious, right?. They both nearly caused death to appear and bitch slap them!

"It's no joke. You know the rules and Patrick will learn them very quickly. Now, before you end up saying something you'll quickly regret, I suggest you go upstairs and chill out in your room." Stavros' voice was extremely stern and Ash swore he saw his father's hand twitching, as if it was ready to reach for his belt just in case Ash's mouth moved faster than he could think.

"Yes, sir." Ash said with a defeated sigh. He clenched his jaw as he turned away and took the stairs two at a time just to get up to his room faster.

Patrick grumbled. "Do I have to stay here?" "Yes," Stavros and Tyler said at once.

"When did you both become my dad to tell me what to do?" Patrick's voice was filled with annoyance.

"The moment I had to feed you" Tyler spoke at the same time Stavros said,

"The moment you decided to act like a child." Stavros stood from his seat so he could start putting the food away as he continued to speak.

"Relax. Ash is a good kid. It'll be fine. He's grounded right now so he isn't allowed out of his room except for school and meals. All you have to do is make sure he stays in his room and keep him alive."

"You say he is a good kid, but urm… last I checked, good kids don't end up grounded" Patrick scoffed. "Besides you wanting me to, not only keep it in the house, but I need to keep it alive?Why are you torturing me like this!" Patrick groaned, reaching up to rub his face.

Tyler laughed. "Relax Patrick. Him being grounded is good because it means he'll stay in his room all day and you can ignore him or pretend he doesn't exist." Tyler stood from his seat and started to wash the dishes.

"You do have to feed him…" Stavros reminded him. "I can't cook!" Patrick hissed.

Tyler laughed again. "Yeah, you really don't want him to try cooking." "How did you manage to live all these years without cooking anything?" "I live with Tyler… He cooks." Patrick shrugged.

Stavros sighed. "Well luckily for you the leftovers from tonight's meal will last for a day or two and if it doesn't I have fixings for sandwiches in the fridge so use that."

Tyler smirked. "You really trust him alone with your son?"

"No. Not at all." He said with a sarcastic smile that was a little too real, "However this is a favor for you two that I am doing and I can't bring Ash with us nor can I leave him home alone because he might actually burn down the house so one of you two are going to stay here with him," Stavros responded.

Tyler and Patrick looked at each other, then looked back at Stavros. "And you thought the best choice was Patrick?"

"Why does it have to be me?" Patrick whined.

Both questions came at once. Stavros rubbed his temples and sighed. "Patrick has always done better with children, oddly enough."

"He doesn't even like children!" Tyler laughed out.

Stavros glared at him. "At least he won't order strippers to keep the kid busy while you go out!" "That happened once! One time!" Tyler huffed.

"The child was six," Stavros said with a heavy sigh.

"Hey he was smiling the whole time!" Tyler narrowed his eyes as he spoke.

"It was a girl." Stavros was getting a headache. The strippers hadn't been happy being lied to and had strong words with Tyler when he returned.

"Patrick may lack the cooking skills, but at least he pretends to be friendly…" Stavros said. He finished up in the kitchen and walked to the living room to sit down.

Patrick blinked. "I pretend to be friendly?" He did a fake sniffle, feigning hurt. "I'm always friendly"

Tyler frowned. "He taught an eleven year old every swear word he could think of two days ago and he keeps handing out scissors and telling the kids to run as fast as they can."

Stavros groaned. "Seriously, Patrick?" He sighed. How can two grown men act like young teenagers? "Maybe I'll just stay home and you guys can go…" He muttered.

"You know we can't go unless we have you or Killian and he isn't around here right now so that just leaves you. Patrick can stay with Ash and take care of him, hopefully without killing him, and you and I will go." Tyler replied. He sat down on the chair and glared at Patrick. "Don't kill him." His voice was stern as he pointed at him.

"You guys take all my fun away." Patrick sighed out. "I guess we're staying here for the night?" He asked.

Tyler nodded. "If Stavros is okay with it, yes."

"That's fine. I don't have a spare room but I can set up the game room for the night for you two," Stavros offered. He did have a spare room but he never got around to getting rid of Ash's baby stuff. He also had a few exercise equipment that was buried but he just wanted to go to bed and not deal with that hassle tonight.

The two nodded.

They talked for another hour or so before Stavros got them set up with some blankets and pillows in the game room. It had a pull out couch in it, though neither one seemed thrilled about having to share a bed. The room had a tv sitting on an entertainment unit with a few different consoles, rows of video games, and even a few board games. There was a white hatch door that led into the basement in the left corner that had a railing around it to keep the two, overly clever, teens from jumping on it. Stavros had built that hatch door when Ash and Liam fell down those stairs one too many times.

Stavros bid them goodnight and headed up to his own room to sleep. He wouldn't deny he was nervous about leaving Ash alone with Patrick because of how great they got along but he trusted Pat to keep Ash alive until they returned.

☽ CHAPTER FIVE ☾

Ash was awoken at five in the morning by his father, who was just waking him to inform him that he and Tyler were leaving now and reminded him to behave and listen to Patrick. He also made sure to let Ash know about the leftovers and sandwich fixings, making sure he knew that Patrick wasn't allowed to use the oven for any reason. Stavros also, begrudgingly, gave his son his cell back but only for emergencies and made it well known he'd be checking to make sure Ash wasn't on it for any other reason.

"Go ahead and go back to sleep. There was a snow storm last night so school was canceled." Stavros hushly said while patting his head.

Ash was thrilled for half a second before remembering he was grounded so he couldn't even enjoy a snow day. Giving his dad a hug, he told him to be careful driving in the snow before turning over to go back to sleep.

Ash had no idea how long he slept for but he woke up smelling something burning and hearing Patrick cursing as the fire alarm went off. He groaned as he stumbled out of bed and made a face as the smell of smoke hit him as soon as he opened his door. He headed to the bathroom before making his way downstairs and saw the house was filled with black smoke and the smell… He had no idea what it even was from.

"What are you doing?" Ash coughed out. He opened the back door quickly and grabbed a dish cloth to wave the smoke away from the fire alarm.

"I was making breakfast," Patrick said with a smile. "I think it's ready now." He sounded way too happy about this.

Ash took a moment to get over being stunned. "I think it was ready ten minutes ago. What are you even making?"

"I was heating up some of the supper from last night." Patrick shrugged. "Tyler told me to just use the microwave." He added.

Ash walked over to it and blinked. "How long did you put it in for?" Whatever was on that plate was charred so badly it was impossible to identify had Patty not told him.

"Oh I don't know. I pushed a few buttons and sat down to watch tv and then suddenly smoke started going everywhere…"

"What buttons did you push?" Ash asked cautiously.

"Um… I think the five, three, maybe the eight and six?" Patrick shrugged again. "Is it supposed to be this black? It didn't look like this last night…"

"How… what?" Ash tried wrapping his mind around this. His father left this guy here to watch him? Really? The guy couldn't even use the microwave properly!

"No it's not supposed to be this black… You're only supposed to put it in for a minute or two." Ash explained, still shocked at the manner of how this person survived, ever. Happily the smoke was slowly clearing out and the stupid alarm stopped blaring. "Have you never used a microwave before?"

"Nope," Patrick still sounded way too happy. "Tyler tried teaching me this shit but it's all too complicated." He sighed. Patrick was thrilled he was even able to figure out how to open the microwave.

Ash grumbled and carefully used the dish cloth to get the plate out of the microwave and set it aside so it could cool down before throwing it out.

Ash muttered under his breath as he got another plate out and put some food on it. "Okay so when you use the microwave to heat something up just put one minute to start. Okay? If it's still cold then add another minute to it." He explained.

Patrick tilted his head as he watched Ash heat up the food. He made it seem so easy but the boy probably used this often so of course he'd know how it worked.

Ash finished heating up the plates of food and sat at the table across from where Patrick sat. It was weird being here without his dad and he was a bit upset that his father didn't trust him enough to leave him alone for a few days but on that same note, Ash knew it was because he caused enough trouble as it was even with his father around.

"So how old are you?" Ash asked.

"Twenty five. How old are you?" Patrick spoke without even looking at the boy. He used his hands this time to eat his food. It was… Odd.

"I'm sixteen.." Ash said. "How are you that old and don't know how to use a microwave?" He asked curiously.

"That old?" he echoed, offended. "25 isn't that old!" If only Ash knew. "I moved around with Tyler a lot. He always did the cooking." Patrick explained with a light shrug.

"He never taught you to use silverware?" Ash asked. He hadn't met any grown ups who used their hands to eat roast. "Did you not have parents or something to teach you this shit?" he asked, dumbfoundedly.

Patrick grinned and looked up from his plate. "Yes, he tried teaching me, but I guess I'm too stubborn because I never caught on to it." He ignored the question about his parents.

Ash cocked an eyebrow at him, stubborn? More like an utter moron. Instead of diving down that rabbit hole, he just gave a nod and went back to eating. He really hoped the place didn't get burned down while his father was away and now he understood his father's warning of not letting Patrick use the oven. Ash would be sure to let it be known that Pat wasn't allowed using the microwave either. Ash was starting to really think about who was babysitting who.

"So, Stavros told me you are grounded" Patrick stated, he then smirked. "What did you do?" "I broke into the old asylum," Ash said with a slight shrug.

Patrick choked on his food as he burst out laughing. "It isn't funny," Ash muttered.

Patrick shook his head. "I highly disagree." He laughed out. "That is fucking awesome." Ash smiled slightly and shrugged again. "My dad didn't think so."

"Yeah well he has a stick up his ass."

It was Ash's turn to choke on his food. "What?" He coughed out, patting his chest hard and grabbing his water to take a sip.

Patrick shrugged. "It's true. Teenagers always do stupid stuff and teenage boys seem to do really stupid stuff as often as possible. It shouldn't be surprising to him that you would do something that stupid." Patrick chuckled. "So what was it like?"

"It was dark… Kinda creepy." Ash shrugged. "We didn't really get far because my dad showed up shortly after we got in."

"We?" Patrick asked.

"My best friend, Liam, was with me." Ash responded. "Liam? Liam Tase?" Patrick asked.

"You know him?"

"Yes. Tyler is making arrangements to get Dan into rehab for his drinking. Liam is going to be staying with me while that happens because his mother didn't seem thrilled with the idea of Liam staying with her." Patrick explained. He had already met the family a few days ago. Liam seemed shy and quiet at first and his mother seemed a little too thrilled about being rid of Liam while Dan was in rehab. Patrick didn't understand the family whatsoever but Liam had agreed to it all.

"His dad agreed to go to rehab? Really? Liam's been trying to make that happen for a few years now," Ash said. It was a little confusing but it also made Ash sad that his mother didn't want Liam around. He never understood how people like Liam's parents could ever have children. "He refused at first." Patrick said. "It took a lot of convincing on Tyler's part but since Tyler promised he was paying for all of it, Dan agreed. It's where Tyler and Stavros went. The rehab is four hours away from here and for the first few days they have to stay there to make sure everything goes smoothly," Patrick explained.

"Where is Liam now? Since you're here with me." Ash asked.

"He is at home packing a few things and staying with his mother until I leave here. I'm taking him back to the motel. He'll take a few days to settle and get use to everything going on so he'll be out of school for the week."

Ash remained silent for a few minutes. He was happy that Dan was getting help but at the same time he was bummed out that he wouldn't see Liam in school for a week. How was he supposed to get by in school if he couldn't hang out with his best friend? Sure he had other friends but still…

Ash cleaned up the dishes once they finished eating and sighed. "Well I'm going back to my room now... I guess," he murmured.

Patrick nodded. "I'd let you hang out down here but if your dad ever found out he may just beat my ass for it so… Have fun being bored in your room."

Ash grumbled and walked up a few steps before pausing and looking at Patrick as he headed towards the living room. "If you need help cooking anything… Just ask okay? If you have no idea how to use it, don't just try using it." With that he headed to his room.

Patrick grumbled as he flipped through the channels on the TV, but it was beyond boring. How did people do nothing but watch TV all day? He didn't get it. "Well might as well take a nap," he muttered. He was supposed to stay inside all day and do nothing? This was the worst kind of punishment ever. He'd rather take an ass whipping any day instead of being grounded for a day, let alo e a week. Instead of just sitting there he decided to get up and just explore the house.

Nothing was all that interesting inside the house but he knew even if he tried laying down to nap he'd get so bored of it and end up staring at the wall the whole time. "I hate you, Stavros" he murmured to himself. "Next time just spank the kid and be done with it." he sighed. This was why he didn't have children. Well okay, so he had many reasons why he didn't have children, one is because he hated kids. He knew how to sort of act around them but those tiny little annoying things were boring.

"At times like this, I wished my house was haunted." Ash murmured, laying on his bed. Remembering his father returned his cell, he grabbed it off the nightstand and opened up the ghost app, mainly just for shits and giggles. He sat up with a flicker of excitement seeing the blip of a ghost somewhere in the house but seeing it jump from one room to another, he sighed. "I knew this app was useless." He closed the app, put his phone down to lay back on his bed. He tossed and turned on his bed but he couldn't relax enough to sleep. This was going to be a very long three days, it was going to be even longer at school without Liam.

☽ CHAPTER SIX ☾

Ash had no idea how much more he could take from Patrick. His father and Tyler were supposed to, hopefully, show up at some point today. He really hoped it happened sooner than later, because he was sure he was close to killing *that* thing. Ash ended up making all their meals because Patrick tried to heat up a sandwich, he had no idea why he tried doing it and when he asked all Patrick said was 'I'm making a hot sandwich'. Ash was sure this guy would be dead if it wasn't for his brother that cooked all their food. He also discovered that Patrick liked doing a lot of weird things, like blaring weird music and singing as loud as he could, or yell at random things if they 'disobeyed' him. Patrick also liked to sleep naked, which scared the crap out of Ash when he woke up at night to go to the bathroom only to find Patty already in there using it.. With the door wide open… naked. Ash would have that image burned into his brain for the rest of his life.

Ash never thought he'd live the day where he was excited to go to school, the place of endless lessons that slowly sucked his soul out, but even school granted him sweet freedom from his boring room and the madness of the adult child he was clearly meant to babysit. His only fear was he'd no longer have a house to return to after school. He did think ahead though and made a few sandwiches for Patty so the man child didn't starve.

It was already the last class of the day, why did school go by quickly when he was grounded but dragged on for years when he wasn't? Some kind of weird witchy bullshit was going on with that. It was his third year in this school and his English teacher still couldn't pronounce his name. She always said 'Ash-ten' instead of 'Ash-ton' and he even told her to call him Ash, like all his other teachers, but he knew she was doing it on purpose because she refused. As pay back, he started to say her name wrong every time she said his wrong. She didn't seem happy about it but he didn't care, he figured he could play this game too.

Ash watched the clock on the wall, only ten minutes left of class. Great, He wasn't really in a rush to get home and back to his room.

"Please be home.." he whispered to himself. He wasn't sure he could last another hour alone with crazy Patrick and he really was judging his father's choice of friends.

Ash sighed hearing the bell ring and gathered up his books before he left the room. He stopped at his locker for a minute to grab his bag and then started walking home. He only lived a few blocks away from his school so walking wasn't all that bad but he did drag his feet as much as he could.

"Oh surprise, surprise. It's still standing." Ash said as he approached his house. He felt disappointment rise in him seeing his father's car wasn't there yet. He groaned in annoyance hearing the loud music playing. He had no idea what Patrick was listening to but it sounded like a dying cat singing and it wasn't pleasant. He walked inside, letting out a breath of relief seeing Patrick actually wearing clothes, and pulled off his shoes before he headed straight up to his room. Patrick had yelled something to him but he didn't bother checking what it was.

Ash stayed in his room while he worked on his homework, rolling his eyes when he heard Patrick yelling at something again.

It was a few hours later when he finally heard the music turn off and realized he heard people talking downstairs. He smiled as he quickly left his room and went downstairs and saw his father with Tyler in the living room.

"At least he didn't burn down your house." Tyler chuckled, standing in the living room.

"Yeah, that's great, instead he decided to move all the furniture out of the living room to dance?" Stavros sighed. He was tired, the trip had been long and tiring and now he had to fix his living room.

"He almost burned down the house." Ash said, stepping into the living room.

"Yeah, sounds about right," Tyler signed, all his faith in Patty instantly vanishing. "Well let's leave Patrick, before Stavros decides to rip your arms off." he chuckled.

"At least *that* is still alive.." Patrick said, lazily gesturing to Ash. "It didn't starve or anything." He smiled. Ash wasn't sure why he sounded so proud of that, he didn't starve to death because he cooked his own meals.

"That's a plus." Stavros grumbled. He walked them to the front door and opened it "Well thank you, Patrick, for keeping my son alive." he said.

Patrick shrugged and as he went to walk out of the house, he paused to turn back to Stavros, "Oh, by the way, I'm sure this isn't important but the annoying thing did try to sneak out the other night to go see his friend."

Stavros instantly looked like he was two seconds from killing the boy, "What? For fucksakes, You had one job!"

"Actually, I had two jobs. Since he is still alive, I'd say that's 50% of a job well done." Pat said, almost cheerfully.

Stavros took a step forward, ready to put Patrick eight feet under, but Pat scrambled behind his brother for cover as a squeak of fear left him.

"We're leaving!" Tyler said quickly, not even giving anyone time to say a word as he grabbed Pat's arm and forced him to start walking away from the house.

Ash was so pale he was sure he was see through, stepping back when he saw that murderous glare on his fathers face when the man turned to him.

"Are. You. Fucking. Serious." Stavros snarled each word.

"Before you become too angry, here is this" he hands his dad a paper with a fake bill on it "For the emotional damage of leaving me in a house with that! I saw him naked" he shivered "It was horrible, like a dwarf walking out of a forest! And don't get me started on the music."

The anger coming from his father was so strong, it was like the house grew colder and darker. "Go to your room. Right fucking now." His voice clearly conveyed he was beyond pissed.

"Let me explain, I had to escape! He almost burnt down the house and the only reason I'm alive is because I know how to use a microwave! He yelled at your tv like some... king because it wouldn't work! I was losing my mind dad!"

Stavros' eyes narrowed the more he listened to his son and he didn't even bother taking the 'bill' from him.

"Ashton Nole Morana, if you plan on seeing your next birthday, you'll go to your room before I drag you up there."

Hearing his full name, Ash dropped the 'bill' and went up to his room so fast, he was on his bed before the paper even touched the floor.

Stavros reached down and jerked the paper off the floor before he went into his office, slamming the door hard enough to shake the whole house and make Ash jump.

Stavros looked over at his son 'bill' as he brewed a cup of coffee, needing it to bring back his sanity. With a heavy sigh, he sat at his desk once the coffee was ready and raised a brow as he looked over the bill.

RECEIPT

MORANA BABYSITTER

2424 Saint Angels St
Redwater Springs

Adult baby child	New cell phone
Fear for life	A car
Keeping house standing	No chores for three years
Teaching man child how to operate a microwave	$500.00
Seeing him naked	$50,000 Non Negotiable
Being Traumatized	New PlayStation
Bleach	$2.00
Emotional Damage	New Gaming Laptop
Ear Damage	The Expensive bluetooth earbuds

Total: You love your son

OR

You can let me go from this prison seeing as I wasn't informed I'd be babysitting that monster of a man. #FREEASH

OR

No further punishment for sneaking out. Please.

THE CHOICE IS YOURS. CHOOSE WISELY.

The more Stavros read, the more amused he got. A smirk grew on his lips and he actually found himself letting out a small chuckle. Rolling his eyes, he read the bottom.

THE CHOICE IS YOURS. CHOOSE WISELY.

Stavros actually laughed, oh, the audacity of this boy. He did have to give him props though on his well written bill and the fact it was able to calm his anger so well.

Finishing his coffee, he took the paper and left his office to head up to his son's room. A low laugh escaped him seeing a note on his door,

"Boycotting free babysitting"

It was clear Ash didn't fully understand what it meant to boycott something, but Stavros wouldn't bring that up.

Keeping a straight face, he knocked on his son's door, only opening it after Ash called out. "Come in"

Leaning against the doorframe after pushing the door open, he held up the bill in two fingers and wiggled it slightly, "Gave this a lot of thought, did you?" he asked.

Ash slowly turned in his chair to face his father, "Yes, father, and it's non negotiable." He crossed his arms over his chest, being very serious.

Stavros held back his amusement, "Well, to start, I'm your father so you don't actually have ground to stand on with what is and isn't negotiable." He began to fold up the paper to slip it into his pants pocket.

Ash gasped, "I almost died! You left me alone for three days with that... that... I can't even think of a word strong enough to describe such a monstrous thing!"

Stavros' cracked a smile, "Oh, I sincerely apologize." he couldn't hold back his laughter any longer. He laughed for a good minute or two before he finally calmed himself enough to speak, "How about you explain to me why you decided to sneak out, after three warnings to behave, and I'll decide from there what to do." he said, sobering.

Ash let out a sigh in relief and relaxed when his dad started laughing. Good, he wasn't pissed anymore, that coffee must be really strong to calm that rage.

Looking down at his hands, he gave the faintest of shrugs, "Patty mentioned that you guys took Dan to rehab and knowing how Lucy is with Liam, I just wanted to check on him, you know?." He paused for a moment, his eyes slowly looking back up to his fathers face.

"Liam was so happy and excited last time, I didn't want him to get too hopeful about it because I knew how badly it'd crush him." he finished, his voice a soft whisper.

Stavros pushed off the door frame and sat down on the edge of Ash's bed. "I hadn't wanted you to know about that yet." he said, sighing at the thought of how he was going to kill Patrick next time he saw that shithead.

Stavros stayed silent for a moment, watching his son closely but he couldn't stay mad at him. "Tyler is mostly staying with Dan and keeping a close eye on him while Patrick watches Liam-" "Dad, Liam is going to drive Patrick insane and that psycho is going to end up killing Liam for it. Liam isn't even that great at cooking, and plus he'll be all emotional-" Ash cut in, only stopping with his father held up his hand to silence him. He couldn't even remain sane while around Patty, no way would Liam handle it.

"I will be checking in daily with Patrick and we both can make them meals or have them over a few times so they don't starve." Stavros said, his voice soothing to try calming Ash's nerves. "Why can't he stay here with us like last time?"

Stavros knew that question was coming, "Because last time Liam was frantic with his emotions and caused you both to fight often. Need I remind you I had to buy a new tv because he threw our old one at you?" he asked, raising a brow.

"We know he can't stay with his mother and I wasn't willing to have him go into foster care or deal with children's aid, so, even though you might not like it, this was the best option."

Ash didn't like it at all but what could he do? On a scale of what is stupid and what is not, arguing with his father was pretty high on that list, so he decided not to.

"I'll tell you what, after today, you are no longer grounded." Stavros said, standing up and looking at him seriously, "But I swear to whatever God you believe in, Ash, You won't be sitting for a year if you break the rules again."

Ash smiled wide at that, deciding to accept the win and spun around in his chair as his father walked out of the room. His happiness was short-lived when his thoughts drifted onto Liam. He prayed the rehab worked this time because, deep down, he knew Liam couldn't handle it if not. He remembered when he first found out Liam was being abused because he showed up to his house with a bruised eye and busted lip, Stavros lost his shit seeing it and Liam had to actually beg him not to do anything about it. He didn't listen, of course, but when he brought Liam to the police station he just lied about what was going on. He really hated to talk about his home life and since then Stavros didn't get involved unless Liam actually asked for help. No one could force Liam to admit anything, they couldn't force him to talk to the cops or move away so they just did what they could and made sure Liam knew they were there to help whenever he needed them.

"Where am I? What's happening?" Everything was pitch black. He had to strain his eyes to see anything in the dark room. He heard screaming, a woman screaming, but he didn't know who it was. Where was he again? He jumped hearing the loud crack of thunder, stumbling back into a toy trunk. He frowned as he waited until lightning flashed before he looked around. Everything seemed perfectly fine in the room, nothing tossed over or destroyed but he could hear things being thrown around, heard voices yelling and more screaming. He felt his heart pounding in his chest as he slowly stepped forward towards the door. He realized he was in a bedroom when he ended up stumbling back onto the bed hearing some horrible cry, he assumed the woman made the sound. He gasped for breath, now realizing he was holding it in. Everything was still so black but his hearing now focused on the rain pouring down against the house as everything else fell silent. After a few moments, he heard heavy footsteps, his breathing quickened as he realized they were approaching the room. What was going on? He knew this place but he couldn't remember how he knew it. His breath caught in his throat when he heard the door opening, his eyes wide with fear as he tried making out what was going on. He saw a dark shadow of a man as the door opened and then suddenly the man was rushing towards him "NO!" he screamed.

Ash jumped awake still screaming the 'NO' from his dream, panting, as the nightmare flew through his mind. He didn't understand anything about the dream he had. He knew that place… somehow but he honestly couldn't remember how he knew it. He remembered the screams, remembered the room… it all seemed so familiar and yet he couldn't place any of it. His heart pounded in his ears as he looked around his room, making sure he was safe and no one else was there. Ash ran his hand through his hair, grimacing, feeling it wet with sweat. It took a few minutes for his breathing to calm down and his nerves to relax enough for him to lay down. "Just a dream" he whispered to himself, taking another quick look around his room before he turned to face the wall. "Just a dream." he repeated, needing to reassure himself. He shut his eyes in hopes to sleep again but he already knew it wasn't going to happen. It may have just been a dream but it had felt so real to him for some reason.

☽ CHAPTER SEVEN ☾

That Saturday, Ash was up early and nearly jumping out of his skin in excitement knowing Patty was bringing Liam over. By the sounds of it, Liam was doing okay, not getting too hopeful about anything. Ash was just amazed knowing Pat hadn't killed Liam yet.

Ash was sitting in the game room playing on his playstation to distract himself as he waited for Patrick to bring Liam over.

Liam was staying with Patty in the motel, which Ash didn't like because the east end was a pretty shitty area to be in, but Liam's dad lived there so at least he was around familiar surroundings. The thing that really sucked was Stavros absolutely refused to let Ash walk there because of how bad it was, plus, it was on the news Thursday night that a body had been found in an alleyway. There were no other details about it other than it looked like a murder, maybe a drug deal gone bad? Who knew, but another body had been found Friday afternoon and that had caused everyone in town to slowly start buzzing about it. Sure, they had murders, but something about these ones seemed off.

Ash's thoughts cleared hearing a knock on the front door shortly after lunch and quickly paused his game as he jumped up and ran to the door. He skipped to a stop and swung it open "Liam!" Ash smiled wide.

Liam looked pretty good so far, his hair was longer, which looked a little weird, but he actually looked more relaxed and happy which was great. Liam chuckled and hugged Ash tightly "Is it weird we react this way to seeing each other after five days?" Liam asked.

Ash shrugged as he pulled away from the hug "Probably, but I won't complain if you don't." He stepped aside for them to walk into the house and then closed the door behind them.

After removing their shoes, Patrick went to the living room as the two retreated to the game room.

"So how are things going?" Ash asked. "You look okay. Patrick is feeding you and everything?" Liam laughed, "No, Patrick doesn't cook. I mean he can, over an open flame, if he actually tries to but it's pretty much me that cooks everything other than when Tyler is around but he spends a lot of time helping my dad."

"Patrick hasn't driven you crazy?" He asked, sitting in his spot on the couch.

"Oh yeah, he has, I don't know what music he listens to but it's horrible and I discovered that he really hates clothes. Tyler yelled at him a few times because Patrick magically "forgot" he wasn't alone in the room and decided to walk around naked." Liam shuddered at the same time as Ash, who remembered the horrible sight. " I know I'm quiet but damn I didn't realize it was so easy to forget I was around." Liam jokingly laughed, as he sat down on one side of the couch. "Other than that, and his annoying habit of always yelling at shit, everything is fine. I get to see my dad in a few days so I'm excited about that. Tyler informed me he was doing really well so far." He automatically grabbed the other controller.

"That's good. I was a little worried about that." Ash admitted, he was actually a lot worried but he didn't want to dwell on that. "Hopefully soon he can come home," he said with a smile, grabbing his controller and unpausing the game.

Liam nodded, "I'm hoping so. I'm grateful the brothers have been really helpful but I do miss being at home in my own bed. I discovered that Tyler is a huge clean freak because Patrick decided to dirty every dish before he returned and then I got to listen to them yell at each other for an hour before Tyler came and scolded me for not keeping things clean." Liam let out a snort, "As if I'm supposed to be Patricks babysitter or some shit."

Ash let out a long, tired sigh, and was starting to see why his father sighed a lot, "Yeah, I realized pretty quickly that Patty can't even watch a rock without it somehow dying." he smirked, "I gave my dad a babysitting bill and that's how I happily got ungrounded." he said with a small laugh.

"I seriously need to write up a bill for Tyler then because having to be stuck suffering with Patrick's stupid ass is a nightmare." Liam was dead serious too. He'd write a long bill, which would honestly be more like a ten page essay.

"How is Liam doing?" Stavros asked. He sat on his couch holding a cup of coffee while Patrick sat on the chair sipping water.

"How can you stand the taste of that shit?" Patrick made a face of disgust.

Stavros looked down at his coffee, a flicker of undying love flashed over his face, "Don't be hating on my coffee. I'm raising a teenager. It's the only thing keeping me sane."

Not wanting to even touch that conversation, or comment on the odd look in Stavros' eyes, he answered his question.

"He is doing alright. He has some down moments but he is really trying hard to work through everything. He finally opened up and told me all about his life and I think that helped." Patrick hadn't cared or even asked for any of that information but he understood people got emotional at times. "He doesn't carry that stress with him anymore which means he is a lot more relaxed so he doesn't get all jumpy when Tyler and I yell around him." Patrick replied. "The plan is going smoothly, a lot easier than I had thought it'd be."

Stavros nodded, "That's good. A boy his age shouldn't be worrying about any of this stuff." The boy getting better was good, as long as Dan didn't fuck this up.

"Has his mother come to see him at all? Or even reach out?"

Patrick shook his head sadly, "Liam tried a few times to get in touch but she only answered the phone once and that was basically to tell him to go pound sand." Patrick shifted in his chair, "It did crush him however he also didn't seem overly surprised which kind of concerned me. She really seems to want nothing to do with the kid. I can understand her keeping distance from his father, but surely she can't be this heartless towards her son." Patrick said, pausing to look at Stavros, "Can she?"

Stavros' lip twitched up into a snarl, "All I know is she'll tolerate Liam for a short time but for some reason she really dislikes him. Which is sad because Liam is a great kid and deserves to be loved, not hated by his own mother." Stavros growled some. He'd never understand that woman but if she was going to treat Liam like a pest, she should have given him up the moment he was born.

"Anyways, be cautious, two bodies have been found murdered not too far from that motel. It might be a good idea to relocate away from that area." Stavros said, changing the topic.

"I'll keep that in mind." Patrick said. "I could move closer to the middle, maybe the west end?" "No," Stavros said firmly. "There's nothing interesting in the West end, you and Liam might actually kill each other in boredom"

"Fine. We'll stay at the motel for now but if things get worse, we'll move." Patrick said, figuring that was a good compromise.

Stavros partly rolled his eyes but accepted that for now.

The two talked for an hour or two, deciding to leave the teens alone for now to unwind and enjoy each other's company, and then got up to go cook dinner. Patrick didn't really help all that much, but only because Stavros adamantly refused to let him. So he just decided to bother the man about how he was cooking everything wrong.

Stavros was five seconds away from giving his bread knife a new purpose when the boys entered the kitchen.

"Good, just in time for dinner," and to save Patrick's life but Stavros didn't say that out loud. He poured the stew in all their bowls and made sure there was enough buttered bread before he took his seat.

Once the other three sat, he spoke, "So, as you both know, there have been some murders" he started. He glanced at the two boys, "That means from now on, no walking around late at night, no sneaking out, none of that shit."

"Do they know any details yet?" Ash asked, knowing this was absolutely a line he couldn't cross. "It seems some people got tired of others living." Patrick said helpfully.

Stavros glared at Patrick but spoke to Ash, "No, they haven't released any."

"Do they know who?" Liam asked. He was silently praying Ash didn't get any smart ideas. Stavros shook his head, "They haven't said." he replied.

Ash had no idea how he was supposed to feel about this. Sure, he knew murders happened a lot around the world but it was rare here. Yea, people got stabbed or shot but it was never fatal, mostly just drug dealers teaching a client or two a lesson on payment but murdered?

"I know you boys are afraid." Stavros spoke softly, seeing the fear in their eyes. "You have a right to be afraid, just remember this fear you get the bright idea to sneak out of the house." Ash gave a nod but he remained silent. What if someone broke into their house to kill them? What if they waited for Stavros to leave and then attacked? Ash had to clear his head because he knew he'd get himself all panicked if he kept on with these questions. He couldn't change any of this and had no control over it but he could at least try keeping himself safe and staying close to home.

Liam also remained silent as he went over Stavros' words. Murders did happen, they all knew that, but this many murders in such a short time? Here? It seemed odd. Someone was definitely after revenge or some serial killer. Liam had caught him briefly wishing his mother went out late at night. Liam was shocked about that thought and wondered if he truly wished that. Sure she wasn't a nice woman but did he actually want her to die? Liam looked up, his eyes locking with Patrick's for a moment and he saw a small grin form on Patrick's face, as if the man had actually heard Liam's thought. He gripped his spoon tightly as he glared down into his bowl at such a nasty thought. He relaxed his grip and began to eat the stew, not looking up at anyone.

Ash cocked his head seeing the grin on Patrick's face and wondered what the hell that was about, he was even more curious seeing Liam glaring down at his bowl but decided, for now, he'd just focus on his own food.

Liam woke up the next morning hearing someone walking around the kitchen. He planned on staying in bed to get some more sleep but once the smell of breakfast hit his nose, he got up and changed into clean clothes. He walked out of the room and down the stairs, smiling seeing Stavros there.

"Need any help?" Liam asked softly, stretching with a yawn as he walked into the kitchen. Stavros glanced over his shoulder at Liam and nodded "You can set the table." he replied with a smile.

Liam nodded and got out some plates and got some glasses of juice onto the table. "I'll go get Ash up." Liam said. He walked up the stairs and knocked on Ash's door. "Hey lazy butt breakfast is almost ready," he called through the door.

Ash groaned as he heard the knock and slowly stood up, yawning as he pulled on clean clothes and opened the door, "You're a lazy butt." he grumbled heading to the bathroom while Liam headed back downstairs.

Ash joined his father and Liam a few minutes later. They all seemed way too tired to talk about anything so they ate in silence and then cleaned up the dishes. Ash thought about just going back to bed but it was Sunday today and he didn't want to waste the weekend sleeping.

"Can Liam and I go to the mall today?" Ash asked. He finished cleaning the counters and looked over at his dad.

Stavros thought for a few moments and hesitantly nodded knowing he couldn't keep the boys inside all day.

"Yes, you two can go," he said. "But be home before 4," he added quickly.

Ash and Liam agreed quickly and took off to get their shoes on and ran out the door before Stavros changed his mind.

Stavros sighed and shook his head with a light chuckle. He walked to his office and decided to do some work but he didn't even get three feet into his office before his cell rang. He checked the number and answered it.

"What's up, Tyler?" he asked, then winced hearing yelling in the background.

"Oh nothing much. Just dealing with an angry Dan." Tyler sighed. "He is about to be kicked out of rehab if he doesn't get his anger under control but I doubt that will happen."

"You could always actually help him instead of just being there." Stavros said. He rolled his eyes as he sat down at his desk "He has only been there a few days. They can't kick him out for being angry. I'm sure a lot of drunks get a little upset when they are told they can't have any more alcohol."

"True, however, at least they don't go around punching random people and threatening to murder the next dumbass that tells him to calm down." Tyler replied.

"Anyways I thought you might want to know about this because if Dan gets kicked from this rehab he'll go back to drinking like crazy and Liam will go into the system since his mother is being a worthless bitch."

"Liam can't go into the system." Stavros said quickly, He knew Ash would freak out if that happened and Liam would just fall apart. Stavros knew the system was useless most of the time. Sure, they helped families but they also ruined families. Stavros would try keeping Liam under his roof but he doubted it would be allowed. He wasn't family but he supposed he could always call in some favors… he did know a few people who could pull some strings.

"The system would just ruin Liam. Just.. calm the man down and fix things. He has to finish that rehab. It's only for two? Three? Months?"

"Two months. It only goes longer if he drinks while here but I don't see that happening since he isn't allowed to leave the grounds."

"Two months doesn't seem all that long.." Stavros murmured.

"It's the typical amount. They can be in here for up to 90 days." Tyler replied. "But everyone seems hopeful that Dan will only need two months so that's what they are trying for. Right now it doesn't seem like that'll be long enough but once he actually gets over the withdrawals and such he should mellow out."

"Then you keep him there until that happens. If he tries threatening anyone else, or even goes to punch someone, knock him out. Okay? Liam has so much faith in this working that he doesn't need to be disappointed if it fails. Don't let it fail." Stavros ordered.

"Fine. I'll put in more effort." Tyler sighed. "I'll call-HEY!

"Liam's doing okay?" Patrick's voice suddenly asked on the other end.

Stavros rolled his eyes, "I am capable of taking care of a child. I don't know if you noticed this or not but I have actually raised one."

"Only for ten years. That doesn't count."

Stavros narrowed his eyes as he tried thinking over this logic. "How many kids have you raised? Cause last time I checked you don't have any kids."

"Well not that I know of anyways. Chances are I have a million right now and it's my great genes that raise them well."

"I can't lower myself down to your level of stupidity." Stavros said. "How you managed to live this long is amazing."

"Tyler takes great care of me." Patrick chuckled.

Stavros rolled his eyes, "Liam is fine and alive. I hadn't realized you cared so much." Patrick snorted, "I don't care."

"Then you're asking… ``why?"

Patrick sighed heavily, "Well no one would trust me to watch their little creatures if word got out that one died… duh."

"Little creatures?" Stavros repeated slowly. "I think that's one of the nicest things you've ever called children."

"For some weird reason parents get upset when I call them 'little pests' or 'rodents'."

"No, really?" Stavros said sarcastically. "Who would think that was something rude to call a child?"

"Hey, have you ever met Killian? He calls them worse. Remember when Jaded actually had to shove him away from literally kicking a child through a window? And that was because it laughed." Patrick pointed out.

"Oh, how can I forget.. I had to listen to those two argue about it for five hours afterwards." Stavros groaned. "I had to actually ban Killian from going anywhere near a child… he still refuses to come to my house because Ash is still, and I quote, "too young to tolerate." Good thing he can't stand females almost as much as he can't stand children because his kids would be screwed." Stavros sighed. Some people weren't meant to be parents and Killian was definitely one of them, Patrick was a close second. How anyone got convinced that letting Patrick watch their children was a good idea was beyond him.

He heard a beep on his phone and looked at the incoming call. "Pat, I gotta go. Liam's fine." he hung up before getting an answer.

"Ash?" he asked, once he answered. "What's wrong?" "Dad, you gotta come to the mall." Ash sounded panicked. "Why? What's wrong?" Stavros asked again.

"Liam is freaking out. Just come quick okay?" he hung up before getting an answer.

☽ CHAPTER EIGHT ☾

Ash stood outside, watching Liam pace in silent panic before his friend finally sat down on the bench and started crying into his hands.

The day had started out great, they were walking around one of the shops just checking to see if there were any new games worth buying until Ash spotted Helliana. Liam practically dragged Ash out to go talk to her when suddenly Lucy was there in front of them.

"I cant believe you are here in this fucking place instead of at your fathers side!" she had snapped.

Liam had stepped back from her sudden appearance, "He's in rehab, I can't actually be there with him bu-"

"Yeah, and because you abandoned him there without a second thought, he's at risk of being kicked out!" she had interrupted.

Liam went wide eyed, "What? How do you know that?" he asked.

"That's none of your fucking business. I always knew you were a worthless son. It's clear Dan hasn't been beating you enough for you to be so stupid and worthless!" Lucy screamed.

Liam flinched like her words had slapped him, everyone was staring at this crazy bitch but none moved to intervene. Ash saw the security guard already on their way to stop this.

"What, nothing to say for yourself?" Lucy screamed, her voice echoing in the mall. "Maybe I should beat the shit out of you too so you'd think!" She had raised her hand to strike him, but Ash had quickly pulled Liam back and behind him, his eyes narrowing on the bitch.

"Go jump on a diseased dick, you fucking whore." Ash spat. He felt his anger boiling at this point and his hands were clenched tightly at his sides to keep from hitting her.

The guards came then and dragged Lucy out, who kicked and screamed the whole way out. Ash turned to Liam and saw the look on his friend's face. He saw the tears in his eyes, the pain there, and knew he couldn't say anything to drown out Lucy's words.

Ash had called his father then and gently wrapped an arm around Liam's shoulders to bring him outside.

"What happened?" Stavros asked, as soon as he got out of his car and ran to Ash, who stood outside with Liam. Stavros had no idea what was going on but he spotted Liam and he looked to be physically okay. No blood anywhere, no wounds…

"She was here." Ash said softly. "She …?"

"Liam's mom" Ash whispered. "She saw Liam and just freaked out over nothing!. I guess she got a call from the rehab place, or from Dan, I have no idea, but she knew he was close to being kicked out of it and she just went off on Liam."

"Where is she now?" Stavros growled out. He didn't care if she was a female; he wanted to tear her apart. She had no reason to be freaking out like this on Liam, especially since she wasn't offering any help, It wasn't like Liam had control over this.

"She isn't here." Ash said. "She was screaming so loud that security came and pretty much had to drag her out of here. She kept saying it was Liam's fault that his father was going through all this. She would have slapped him if I hadn't stopped her."

Stavros cursed and walked over to Liam. The poor boy was sitting on a bench with his head in his hands just shaking and he didn't even look up when Stavros sat down beside him. He didn't say anything, he just pulled the boy close and held him. He could hear Liam sobbing but he knew there weren't any words of comfort, not right now, not with Liam being a total mess right now. He'd have to wait for Liam to calm down before the boy would actually listen to anything he said.

Ash stood off to the side and felt like hunting the bitch down and just screaming at her. He had no idea what her issue was but she had no right to just freak out like that, let alone track them down and scream at him.

"Is he okay?" a soft voice asked behind Ash. He turned and looked at the female who spoke, instantly blushing seeing it was Helliana.

Ash opened his mouth to speak but it felt like his tongue swelled up three times its size, his throat closed, and his mouth went dry. How could this happen? Why did this have to happen? "H-h-he um…his mom.. " He stumbled over his words. It wasn't this hard to form words!

Helliana tilted her head as she looked at Liam. She knew them from her history class but she didn't talk to them too much. She honestly didn't talk to anyone. She had friends but even they got annoying to listen to most of the time. She didn't care about who was dating the hottest guy or girl around, or who messed up on a test or who's parents were being unfair. It never mattered to her and all her friends seemed to be stuck up most of the time. She didn't even pick them for friends, they just flocked over to her and never left.

"Are you okay?" She asked. Her voice was soft and sounded so much like an angel… or so Ash thought anyway.

Ash nodded slowly.

"Ash?" Stavros called out softly. He stood with Liam and kept an arm around him as they walked over to Ash and the girl. "I think it's time we go home." Stavros stopped beside Ash and looked at her. He didn't know who she was but judging by how stiff Ash was and the faint blush on his cheeks, he assumed he had a crush on her. "Who is this?" he asked, a slight smirk on his lips.

Ash cleared his throat some, "Oh, this is um… dad this is…"

"Helliana." She giggled softly. Oh jeez she had such a cute giggle! And such cute dimples when she smiled..

"Mr. Morana. I'm Ash's father." He smiled, and extended his hand.

"It's a pleasure meeting you." She said, shaking his hand. "Is Liam alright?" she asked softly. "He's fine. Just had a rough day." Stavros replied. "Well, Ash, we should head home. Helliana, it was nice meeting you." he smiled. He started walking slowly with Liam and glanced back at Ash, who was all but drooling as he stared at her.

Ash waved shyly at Helliana "Bye." he murmured and quickly caught up to his father and Liam. "See you at school!" She called after him, before walking off.

"So who is that?" Stavros asked, a grin on his face.

Ash shrugged some, "She's just a girl in our history class." "Ash's in love with her." Liam chuckled weakly.

"Oh?" Stavros grinned more. "Does she know that?" He asked.

"Shut up, Liam. I'm not in love with her.. I just like her.. She's a nice friend." Ash grumbled, though he could feel his cheeks heating up.

"A nice friend that you never talked to?" Liam teased. "My bad, Hardly, talked to"

"Oh, good god.. You've never spoken to her?" Stavros sighed. He reached up and rubbed his temples. "I've failed as a father. How can my son not know how to talk to a girl?"

Ash rolled his eyes. "Shh! Both of you. I know what I'm doing… you gotta build up to it."

"For three years?" Liam laughed weakly. At least talking about this made him feel a little better though his mother's words still screamed in his head.

"Why does it take three years of build up?" Stavros asked. He found this highly amusing. "It's like foreplay.." Ash said. "You can't just jump into things, you have to do it slowly.."

"I realize you are sixteen but I really don't want to think about my son and the fact that he knows how foreplay works so let's just stay clear of that topic for now." Stavros grumbled. "Wait, Patrick isn't the one who taught you that stuff right?" he asked, narrowing his eyes. He stopped at the car and Liam slipped into the back while Ash sat in the front.

"No, dad, weirdly enough there is this funny class in school… what was it called? Not English" he used his finger to tap his chin in fake thought, "Math? No that doesn't sound right. Oh yeah! It's called sex Ed. They kind of teach that stuff.." Ash said.

Liam laughed in the car.

Stavros kept his eyes narrowed for a minute. He knew Patrick always made his sick jokes or decided that a very detailed picture was needed when talking about his fun sexy time. He also knew that Patrick didn't care at all about young ears hearing.

"Fine, let's go home." Stavros said. He'd drop it. He knew sex Ed was taught in schools. It seemed odd that foreplay was involved but then again they were in highschool. He knew little pricks in high school always talked about their stupid little sex adventures.

Everyone slipped into their own thoughts as Stavros drove them home. Once they returned home, they got inside and the boys started heading upstairs.

"Ash." Stavros said, both boys pausing. "Why don't you go upstairs and Liam will join you in a minute." he smiled. He put his shoes away and hung up his coat. He waved Liam over to him and sighed as he placed a hand on his shoulder. "I don't know what your mother said, I don't need to know. What I do know is that you are a smart young man and are handling everything with amazing strength. Don't listen to her, okay? She doesn't know what she is talking about and she has no right to go off on you like she did." He pulled the boy into a hug, lightly rubbing his back. "One day she'll see the amazing man you become and regret missing all of it."

Liam smiled weakly "Thanks. I'll try okay?" he promised. He wished her words didn't affect him so much but it was his own mother yelling how useless he was, so it did hurt.

"Good. Now you go up and bug Ash while I start lunch." Stavros said. He gently squeezed the boy before releasing him and watching him run up the stairs. He sighed, making a mental note to add that bitch to his list, before he shook his head and he walked to the kitchen to start making lunch.

☽ CHAPTER NINE ☾

"What did he want?" Ash asked, when Liam walked into the room.

Liam smiled some, "He just wanted to help me feel better. Basically just said my mom's a bitch and doesn't know a thing about me so she can't judge me. Just in nicer words." he said, chuckling softly.

"Ah. Well it's true." Ash murmured. "Anyways I saw this new game come ou-"

"No, no. We are not doing that stuff. We are going to talk about Helliana. Dude, it's about time you tried asking her out." Liam cut in. He sat down on the bed and sighed, "You shouldn't put it off forever."

"I can't even say 'Hi' to her. How the hell am I supposed to ask her out?" Ash muttered. "She doesn't even like me. I mean we've been in her class forever and she's never even noticed me until today."

"We haven't been in her class forever. Stop being a baby. If you aren't man enough to try talking to her in person why don't you just try talking to her online instead?" Liam suggested. "It can't hurt."

"What am I supposed to say?" Ash asked.

"How about you start with 'Hey' and see where it goes from there?" Liam suggested helpfully. "I'm not even friends with her on anything."

"There is the school app. Talk to her in that."

Ash narrowed his eyes some but walked over to his laptop and flipped it on. He muttered to himself about Liam being a pain in his ass, as he logged onto the school app and scrolled through the names.

"That is going to take hours. Just search her name. See? Search bar. Right there!" Liam pointed to it, having gotten off the bed to stand beside him.

Ash rolled his eyes as he searched her name and clicked on it to send a message. He tapped his fingers a little on the keys but didn't type anything yet.

"Oh for the love of.. Move." Liam scrowled. He quickly pushed Ash out of the way and began typing.

"Hey!" Ash snapped.

"See, that wasn't so hard to say. You should try saying that to her but maybe with a little less attitude." Liam chuckled. He sent the message and just shook his head as he listened to Ash groaning behind him. "Relax. If we waited for you to grow the balls to do this we'd be waiting for decades." Liam said with a grin.

"I hate you." Ash muttered.

"You love me." Liam grinned, hearing the 'ding' of a new message, he gestured to the laptop, "Hey look. She messaged back. She says hi and everything." Liam said triumphantly. He began typing again and hummed softly to drown out Ash whining behind him. He found it amusing that he freaked out over such a little thing but he couldn't really give him too much trouble over it simply because he hadn't even tried getting to know his little crush.

"Why did you send a winky face? That just makes me seem like a tool." Ash growled some. He was not enjoying this. Not. At. All.

"It shows interest." Liam explained. "You want to give this a shot?" he asked. He didn't bother waiting for Ash to say anything though, he was really focused on the task at hand. Ash needed a date. "Hey, have you given any thought about the annoying school dance for Christmas?" he asked.

"No. Why would I?" Ash asked. Why would he want to attend a dance when he knew he'd end up tripping over his own feet trying to dance?

"Well you just asked Helliana to go with you so you might want to think about going." "What? Are you insane? I can't dance!" Ash hissed in frustration.

"You should consider learning." Liam smiled. "Dude, she actually said yes!" he laughed. "Man, you are screwed now."

"Oh I hate you. Why would you do this to me? I'm going to end up stepping on her feet or tripping her and breaking her back… oh I'm never going to get another date- wait? She said yes? She said yes!" Ash smiled wide, hoving over Liam's shoulder to look at the screen. He couldn't believe she said yes! She actually said yes! A female had agreed to go to a dance with him… and now he suddenly felt sick. Being so excited yet nervous all at once was not a good feeling. He groaned as he staggered over to his bed, plopping down. "This is the worst yet best thing to ever happen to me." he whispered.

"Calm down. We'll figure something out okay?" Liam said, glancing back at him. "Do you know how to dance?"

"Um no, but I'm not going so I don't gotta learn." "Why aren't you going? You can't make me go alone!"

"You aren't going alone, remember? You're going with Helliana. Your date. I'm not going because the rehab is closed for the holidays so my dad is coming home for a few days. Tyler promised me that he'll be in great shape for it. I know I shouldn't get too hopeful, but I'm a little excited for it." Liam said with a shrug. "So I'll be at home with my dad. Patrick and Tyler will be there for a few hours when he first gets home and they have already cleared out any booze from the house. They will also be keeping his money so he can't go out and buy more. If everything goes great he might not even need to go back to the rehab center." Liam smiled. He had to keep reminding himself not to think too much about it or else he'd just get filled with hope. He wanted to hope it all worked out but Tyler had warned him that it might take more time than planned.

He knew it wasn't something that was going to happen overnight or even in a few days but just thinking about his dad sober… he remembered the few times his dad had been sober. The first time was when he was eleven and they went camping. He learned how to fish and they had a blast but that had been his first and only time to ever go camping. His father got sober again when Liam was thirteen and they went to the zoo for the first time, which was great fun, but as soon as they got home his dad started drinking again. His dad had been sober a few other times but that only lasted for a day and the whole time his dad either slept or freaked out over everything because he was craving a drink but had no money for anything.

"That's great. I hope it all works out." Ash smiled. He really did. Sure Dan was an ass but if he got sober and actually stayed sober maybe he'd turn out to be a great dad?. It was something Liam really deserved and he wasn't sure how well things would go if it all failed. He knew his best friend would be crushed.

"I do too." Liam said softly.

"Boys, come down for lunch." Stavros called up. He walked into the kitchen and sighed softly as he sat down.

Ash walked down the stairs and into the kitchen followed by Liam. They both sat down and started to eat away at the leftover beef stew.

Stavros was lost in thought as he ate away at his stew. The two boys talked to each other but he didn't pay any attention to it right now until he heard Liam speaking to him.

Stavros looked up at the boy, "What?" he asked. Liam frowned some, "You okay?" he asked. "Yes." Stavros replied with a fake smile.

Liam chuckled softly, "We were talking about the winter dance that's going on at the school. Ash got a date!"

"Liam!" Ash snapped, wishing he could make him shut up. He stood up to bring his bowl to the sink.

"A date?" Stavros asked. He looked over at Ash, "Who?" "That girl, Helliana." Liam said. "Now Ash is being all pouty."

Stavros raised a brow, "Pouty? For having a date to a dance? I thought people pouted when they didn't have a date? Man, how times have changed.." he said. "What's the problem, Ash?" he asked.

Ash rolled his eyes, "I'm not being pouty, okay?. I am actually really excited for it." he said. "But…?"

"But what?"

"It sounded like the end of that sentence had a 'But' in it." Stavros said. He stood and brought his dishes to the sink and glanced at Ash as he stood beside him. "So?" he prompted.

Ash sighed, "The dance is in two weeks.. I have no idea what I am even supposed to wear" he said.

Stavros chuckled lightly, "A suit?" he suggested. "That always seems to be the best choice. We can go out and get you one." he said. "Do you have a date, Liam?" he asked over his shoulder. Liam shook his head, "Nah. I don't do dances." he said.

"Why not?"

"They are loud and full of stupidly annoying people." Liam stood up and brought his bowl to the sink as he finished his juice. He leaned against the counter and set his glass down, "Don't worry. I have no interest in silly dancing."

Ash narrowed his eyes at Liam, "Why were you so concerned about me going then?" he asked. He crossed his arms over his chest and huffed some.

Liam snorted, "So you'd have a girlfriend." he shrugged.

"I only got the girlfriend because you pretended to be me and asked her to the dance." Ash pointed out.

"I'm confused." Stavros interjected, before Liam could respond. "Liam's got a girlfriend?" Ash sighed, "No… well yes… sort of.."

"Those are the three options.." Stavros said slowly.

Liam chuckled, "I used his school account to talk to Helliana for him to ask her to the dance. It's his girlfriend. I just got them talking."

"Ahhhh" Stavros said in one long breath.

"Ash not having a suit isn't even his biggest problem though." Liam said. "Shh." Ash hissed out.

Liam ignored him. "He doesn't know how to dance." Ash glared at him but he only smiled in return.

Stavros chuckled softly as he shook his head, "That's an easy problem to solve." "How?" Ash asked. "I don't know anyone who can teach me to dance."

Stavros smiled, "Yes, you do." "Who?"

Stavros smiled again and gave a playful bow, "Me, silly." Ash stood shocked while Liam burst out laughing.

☽ CHAPTER TEN ☾

"So what are you going to do?" Patrick asked, looking at Tyler. They sat in a small bedroom in the rehab center. Dan was busy getting sick in the bathroom because he had bribed someone to bring in whiskey for him the night before. The room had a single bed, a small dresser, nightstand, and the bathroom. It was painted in gross pastel colors that made Patrick want to stab himself in the eyes with a rusty fork.

Tyler sighed heavily, "I have no idea." he said.

"Are you going to tell Stavros?" Patrick asked, a slight smirk on his lips.

"Hell no." Tyler growled out. He didn't have to report everything to that man and he honestly didn't want to listen to the guy whine about all of this.

"So what's the plan?" Patrick asked. He knew Tyler had to have some sort of a back up plan. Tyler shook his head as he heard Dan throw up again and wrinkled his nose in disgust. Why would anyone be willing to get drunk if it caused them to be sick the next day? He didn't understand it. "We are going to take him home." Tyler finally answered.

Patrick choked and stared at Tyler, waiting for him to actually explain his suicide plan. "What?" he finally asked, when Tyler remained silent.

"We will take him home and just deal with all this there." Tyler said. "He got kicked out, it's not like we can just hide him here." Tyler sighed. Why did he bother dealing with this? He should have just stayed hidden away.

"What about Liam?" Patrick asked. "I thought we were supposed to be 'helping' them. You know how bad things can get with Liam there and plus Stavros will end up finding out."

"You scared of him?" Tyler asked with a smirk. "You aren't?"

Tyler sat there for a minute and actually thought about that. He had many reasons to fear Stavros but the man wasn't like how he used to be. He actually seemed to...care. Which was sickening and made him seem a lot less scary. "I am scared of him but not as scared as I used to be." Tyler answered.

Patrick snorted a laugh and shook his head, "Not at all comforting."

Tyler ran his fingers through his hair, "It's not supposed to be comforting." he sighed. "I can't convince that annoying shithead to keep Dan here." Tyler did not like the lady who ran this place, Trish, because she acted like everyone was beneath her and she shat gold. He already got into a few arguments with her.

"Well I guess you can get him all packed up and bring him back home. I'll leave and go get Liam." Patrick said. He stood up slowly and stretched, "How will we keep Liam from saying anything?" Patrick asked.

Tyler shrugged as he stood up slowly, "That is something for you to figure out. Now go before Dan leaves the bathroom and starts a fight with you again."

Patrick rolled his eyes as he walked out the door. He already got into two fights with the man over nothing. Dan seemed to just get pissed off anytime Patrick opened his mouth to speak. Patrick walked out to his black mustang muttering to himself as he got in and took off driving. How the hell was he supposed to figure this out? He growled under his breath and clenched his jaw every so often as he tried to think of something.

Tyler finished getting Dan's things together and knocked on the bathroom door, "Dan?" he called out. "It's time to go."

Dan let out a groan but said nothing.

Tyler cursed under his breath and forced the door open. He looked at the pathetic human lying on the bathroom floor covered in sweat and even vomit. He fought the urge to roll his eyes as he knelt down and looked him over, "You're a mess."

Tyler grabbed the man's arm and yanked him up onto his feet as he stood and kept a firm grip on his arm to keep him from stumbling back. He walked Dan out of the bathroom and forced him to sit on the bed.

Tyler worked on changing Dan into a clean shirt, happily the man didn't try fighting against him, and put the dirty shirt into the garbage. He sighed softly as he looked the man over and shook his head, "Lets go." he murmured. He honestly wished he didn't have to deal with such things sometimes.

Tyler walked out of the door with Dan's bag and glanced back just to make sure the idiot was actually following him. He looked bored as he watched Dan stumbling behind him and had the sudden urge to punch him but such things could wait until later he supposed. He didn't need or want Dan bleeding all over his car.

The walk out to the car felt like it lasted for hours, since Dan seemed to have trouble remaining on his feet or even walking a straight line, but Tyler refused to help him any. Tyler got the bag into the trunk of his silver Jaguar and opened the back door for Dan so he could at least lay down and sleep the whole car ride. He got the man buckled in and shut the door, even made sure the child safety lock was on, before he got into the driver's seat and took off to Dan's house. Tyler knew it was clean of any alcohol, even though he didn't really care if Dan went out to buy more, and he'd have to stay close to the house to see how things went. Dealing with drunks was annoying to him but things were going so perfectly with Dan and Tyler knew it wouldn't be long before he got a decent meal.

"I don't think it fits right." Liam said. He was at a tailors shop with Ash and Stavros to get a nice suit all fitted for Ash.

"It's itchy." Ash grumbled. He was not a fan of this at all. Why did he have to wear a suit? Weren't jeans and a shirt good enough?

"Relax, Ash. It looks great." Stavros said. "You are taking a lady to a dance so you have to make sure everything is perfect. It's a big deal for you and her so relax and let the man do his job. He is almost done anyways."

Ash muttered to himself and just stood there as the tailor made adjustments on the black suit. "Alright. I got what I needed. You may change into your clothes but don't knock out the pins or I'll have to do it all over again." The tailor said. He walked over to his desk and started writing things down.

Ash got off the stool and practically ran to the change room. He knew his father mentioned getting a suit but he hadn't realized he would have to actually do it. He shut the door and carefully removed the suit and set it to the side neatly, just to make sure he didn't knock out any pins, and then changed into his own clothes.

Liam slowly paced around the room and looked at all different kinds of fabrics and suits hanging along the walls. The room was in the back of a suit shop just for fittings. It had a red carpet with brown walls, a wall mirror between two dressing rooms, a desk full of papers and a computer, and another door to the bathroom. Liam ate an apple as he walked around and tried not touching anything since Stavros already warned him that he'd get broken fingers if he did.

"How long until it's ready?" Stavros asked the tailor.

"It should be less than a week. I'll give you a call when it's done."

Stavros nodded and waited for Ash to exit the dressing room. He thanked the tailor and walked out of the store with Ash and Liam close behind him. "Alright so that's all done. Should we get some dinner?"

Liam tilted his head, "I would but that looks like Patrick." he pointed ahead of them. Sure enough it was Patrick.

Patrick walked up to them and stopped a few feet from Stavros, "Hey, Stavros." he greeted. Liam smiled as he stepped forward, "How's my dad doing?" he asked, before Stavros could say anything.

Patrick shrugged, "As good as expected I guess. I've come to take you home now." "Home?" Stavros asked before Liam had the chance.

Patrick gave a nod, "Yes. Tyler and I have decided it was time to get Liam back on a normal routine so I will be staying with him at his house and he can go back to school tomorrow." Liam was excited about that, sure school did suck but he didn't want to fall too behind on his school work.

"Well I guess I'll see you tomorrow at school." Ash said with a smile.

Liam nodded and moved to stand beside Patrick, "What about my stuff at Ash's house?" "He can bring it to school tomorrow for you." Patrick replied.

Liam nodded and waved bye to his friend as he followed Patrick out to his car. He got in and smiled as he looked at Patrick, "So what's all going on with my dad?" he asked.

Patrick sighed as he started the car and began to drive, "You'll find out soon enough," he murmured.

☽ CHAPTER ELEVEN ☾

"Why is he home?" Liam practically yelled. He had arrived home with Patrick and discovered that Tyler was back with Dan instead of at the rehab center.

Patrick sighed as he sat on Liam's bed while the boy paced around the room. Liam's bedroom was painted a pale blue and had posters of random things hanging on the walls. He had a single bed with a nightstand beside it that looked like it'd burst apart if touched and a small desk that was messy on top.

"He got kicked out of rehab so Tyler decided to bring him home and try helping him here. Tyler cleaned out any booze laying around and he will be staying here until Dan is able to be alone." Patrick explained.

Liam shook his head, "It's not going to work with him being here. He has to go somewhere else." "Do you have the money for that?"

Liam stopped moving and glared at Patrick, "You guys paid for it once. Why can't you do it again?"

"We aren't made of money," Patrick replied. It was a lie but Liam didn't need to know that. "Just calm down, Liam. Take deep breaths and make yourself relax. It will be more difficult this way but it can work."

Liam rubbed his face and sighed heavily as he flopped down on his bed. He stared at the wall for a few minutes "Why can't I stay with Ash?" he asked softly.

Patrick shrugged, "I'm supposed to be watching you, not pawning you off to someone else, and we weren't planning on telling anyone about Dan."

"Why not?"

"Because something like this isn't going to work if everyone knows about it and comes poking around every five seconds." Patrick explained with a sigh. Why did he have to explain things to a teenager? Couldn't he just sit down and be silent while doing as he is told?

"I'm not supposed to tell anyone?"

"No. Right now Tyler is working on Dan and we don't need Stavros coming here and yelling about all this so for now just keep it to yourself."

Liam gave a nod and sighed. He didn't like keeping anything from Ash. They were best friends and told each other everything but he knew he had to keep this to himself for right now.

Patrick watched Liam for a minute before he stood up and left the room. Things were working out perfectly so far and he knew it wouldn't be much longer before they were ready.

Liam was nervous about all of this and how it'd actually go but he had to have some faith that everything would work out. He knew his father wasn't some horrible guy when he was sober, he was actually kind and encouraging and they did things together.

Liam listened to his father yell at Tyler and bit his lip. He hoped a fight didn't happen. He didn't hear Tyler so he assumed the man was talking. Could this actually work? Did he dare hope it would? He has been let down in the past… Liam shook his thoughts out of his head and decided he just needed to shower and get to sleep and that's exactly what he did.

☽ CHAPTER TWELVE ☾

"Lucian," Stavros said, surprised, as he opened the front door. He stepped back to let the man in.

"I hope I'm not intruding." Lucian said, walking inside. With a grin that reached his hazel eyes, he held up $2. "I heard a certain someone needed bleach," he teased.

Stavros reached up to rub his temples, "Only here for three seconds and already tempting death. You know I got large knives here, right?"

Lucian laughed lowly, "Oh I know, but you love me too much to kill me." he said. He shifted a large box from under his arm and set it on the ground.

"Oh, God. What is that?" Stavros asked, glaring at the box.

"None of your business. It's for Ashy boy." Lucian replied. He removed his jacket and hung it up while saying, "Speaking of which, where is the little demon?" he asked.

"He's-"

"Ashy isn't a little demon, don't be rude, Lucian." Dakota said, walking in behind him. "He's a sweet little angel."

Stavros rolled his eyes at them both, "Fuck, I already need coffee." he moaned to himself. He let out an irritated sigh, seeing Dakota holding not only a big box, but also a container of bleach. "Let me guess," He said, pointing to the items, "Those are for Ashy? The sweet little demon/angel child?" he rolled his eyes again.

"Yes, now where is he?" Dakota asked, shutting the door behind them and removing their shoes.

"Yup, a gallon of coffee." Stavros said. "You two spoil him far too much, no wonder he is being a little shit lately." He spoke as he walked to the kitchen, knowing they would follow.

"Ash went to the mall with Helliana after school." Stavros said over his shoulder. He went straight to the coffee pot to brew himself some fresh coffee, the only thing to ever keep him sane anymore.

"Who's Helliana?" the two asked in unison.

Stavros turned to face them as his coffee brewed, crossing his arms and smirking, "Helliana is his girlfriend."

"Ashy? Having a girlfriend? He's still too young for that!" Dakota said, pouting.

Lucian laughed, "Oh shit, I can't wait for the day he comes home panicking because he got her pregnant."

Stavros actually let out a whimper at that thought, "No, don't curse me like that, as Dakota pointed out, he's a sweet little angel and would never do that."

Dakota took a seat at the table, a slow smirk growing on their face, "Didn't Ash's dad knock up his mom around 16?" they asked.

Lucian held back a laugh at the murderous look that flashed across Stavros' face.

"Why are you both here?" he asked. "And not here as in, this town, but why in my house?" Dakota's green eyes blinked a few times, an innocent smile across their face, "We stopped by to see Ashy." they replied. "You just happen to live here with him."

"Don't piss the man off, Dakota, rumor has it he has large knives." Lucian said with amusement in his voice. He also sat at the table, both of them keeping their gifts for Ash close by so his evil daddy didn't lock them away.

Dakota shook their head, red hair bouncing side to side at the movement, "So, who's this Helliana and how long has Ash been dating her?" they asked, deciding changing topics would be good for their health.

Stavros didn't speak until his coffee was brewed, needing it to keep his patience. Once he poured his cup, he sat down by the two, "She is in one of his classes, I've only met her once but she seemed sweet, maybe a little shy." he said with a shrug, lifting his cup to his lips and taking a big sip.

"You know, the shy girls are the ones to be careful of, right? Isn't it well known they can be a little… adventurous?" Lucian asked, loving to tease Stavros and maybe give him an early heart attack.

Stavros actually spat his coffee out, choking and giving Lucian a glare, "You made me waste a perfectly good sip."

Lucian stood and grabbed a dishcloth to clean up the mess, a small laugh leaving him, "Do you ever drink anything else? I hear juice tastes great, or even water!"

"Juice is too sweet and water is just for cooking." Stavros said, matter-of-factly, "Leave me and my bitter love alone." he said, partly narrowing his eyes at him, "You can have your nasty rock water."

Dakota gave an eye roll, "Anyways," they said, getting both men's attention, "Are you sure it's safe for him to be out? I heard on the news about the two murders the other day."

"He is on strict-"

"Two?" Lucian cut in. "No, it's up to five now. I was walking downtown and everyone was talking about how three more bodies were found."

"What?" Stavros asked, panic showing in his voice.

Lucian nodded as he kept talking, "Yeah. It was behind the mall, actually and-"

"Fuck" Stavros hissed. He stood without listening to another word and was at the front door in a second, rushing to get his shoes on while dialing Ash's cell. "Pick up," he snarled at the phone. "Hey, you reached Ash. I'm not av-"

"Damnit, boy, answer the fucking phone!" Stavros growled, hanging up and redialing his number. He didn't even notice Lucian and Dakota following behind him. He nearly ripped the door off its hinges, yanking it open.

"I'm sure he's fine, Stabby," Dakota said, running to keep up.

"Stay here, Dakota, and call me if he returns. Lucian, go search outside the mall while I go in the mall." Stavros barked the orders out.

Lucian exchanged a glance with Dakota however he didn't argue. He got in his own car and took off.

Stavros nearly tore up his driving, peeling out of it so fast and headed straight for the mall.

Ash was redder than a tomato the whole time he walked with Helliana to the mall. Liam hadn't been in school today and, to Ash's surprise, Helliana came up to ask him if Liam was okay, which he honestly had no clue. He hadn't even answered her question, instead, his dumb mouth decided to startle the poor girl and screamed out, "WANT TO GO TO THE MALL?" Ash could have died right there, in fact, he wished he did.

Helliana, understandably, was taken aback by his sudden scream, but seeing how red he was, she just giggled and gave a small nod.

"That would be wonderful! We can pick out my dress." She exclaimed happily.

Ash couldn't think of a single word to say to her the whole walk to the mall, even in the first store they were in, he was silent. Unlike him, Helliana knew how to speak to another human being.

She had asked him a few little questions and, like the moron he was, he just stumbled out random sounds, not even words! Sounds! But it made her giggle which sounded so adorable. Happily, he managed to remember how to talk.

"Liam is okay, I think." Sure, it was almost an hour ago she asked but.. Oh well.

Ash nodded along as she spoke but he honestly couldn't focus on her words, just how soft and perfect her voice sounded. He helped her grab a few dresses and, like a good boyfriend, he sat and waited for her to try on each one. He gave his honest opinion on each one until she finally stepped out in a red dress that clung to her every curve. His mouth went dry while his eyes slowly took in the image. The v neck was low enough to tease his eyes, but classy and elegant. The slit up the side revealed her leg up to her knee, which was perfect because Ash knew any higher and the school wouldn't let her into the dance, plus, just this sight alone was enough to make him squirm just a little in his seat.

"You look.." he trailed off for a moment, trying to think of the right word to say. Beautiful didn't seem good enough and pretty was just wrong.

"Stunning" he finally said.

Helliana blushed, "Thank you." she replied sweetly. She did a little spin for him and then returned into the room so she could change.

Ash shut his eyes and forced himself to take in a few deep breaths. He needed to calm himself down fast so, regretfully, he forced himself to remember that night he saw Patrick naked.

Relieved that it worked, he reminded himself to get bleach before going home.

Once Helliana was finished changing, they went to pay for the dress and started walking around the mall. Ash was more relaxed now so he was actually able to keep up with conversation, until something horrible caught his eye.

He stopped dead in his tracks, making a face seeing this lady walking towards them with horrible pink hair. By the looks of her clothing, she was a nun, why she had pink hair? He had no idea.

Helliana had noticed he stopped but had no idea why, "Ash?" she asked, slightly concerned. The lady with pink hair looked straight at Ash, like she was staring right into his soul, as she walked. Ash felt that pit in his stomach again, he was frozen in his spot but he wasn't sure why. Was he afraid? Nothing about her seemed threatening except for the way she looked at him, like he was her next meal.

"Nothing is truly what it seems." The pink-haired lady spoke, not once breaking eye contact or even slowing. She just walked right past him, as if she hadn't even spoken to him or saw him. Ash's body turned, his wide eyes still following her, what did she just say? He wanted to call out to her, to demand answers, but he couldn't even open his mouth. It was like everything forgot how to function.

Ash suddenly felt a cold rush run straight through him, right down to his bones. His body was screaming at him to run, that something extremely dangerous was near him and every hair on his body was standing but he didn't understand why. What was going on? He *knew* someone was watching him and it wasn't until he saw the pink-haired lady stop by a man that he finally figured out what sent his body on high alert. The man was tall, about the same height as his father, and had soulless eyes that seemed to glow red. Ash couldn't stop staring at him, the man's skin was so pale it was like he never stepped foot into daylight before. His hair was black with silver highlights, it almost looked like he had blades in his hair but that wasn't what caught his attention about him. Ash noticed the man had a red dragon tattoo on his face, the dragon's head rested above the man's right eye and its body trailed down the side of his face, the tail curling just below his chin. He's never seen someone with that kind of tattoo however, he's never seen this man before. The other thing that caught his eye was the fact that this man had claws instead of fingernails, who the hell had claws!? And to make it worse, they were a deep red, like blood red, as if he just finished tearing people open with them.

"Ash?" he barely heard Helliana calling out to him again. He felt her touch on his arm but he

couldn't look away, it was like his instinct knew he couldn't turn his back on this man. He saw the man smirking at him, flashing something that looked like a fang… fang? No. Fucking. Way. Who had fangs!? Was this man a vampire? He swore the mall actually darkened around him, like there was a spotlight on him and that man. He heard a faint chuckle echo around him, it was deep and threatening, he knew it came from the man. It felt like hours went by with them just standing there, staring at each other, and it wasn't until the man reached up a clawed finger, putting it over his lips in a 'shh' motion, that everything returned to normal. The mall returned to its normal brightness, people were walking around him, buzzing in conversation like nothing happened.

Ash gasped sharply, having not even noticed he had been holding his breath. Panting heavily, he looked around quickly realizing the man and pink-haired lady were suddenly gone.

"Where did they go?" Ash panted out, spinning around like a mad man. "Who?" Helliana asked, even more concerned and looking around.

"That man and lady… they were just right there!" Ash said, pointing to where they had been standing.

Helliana stepped even closer to him, "Ash, are you okay?" she asked, touching his arm again. Ash honestly had no idea if he was okay but before he could answer, he heard his dad's voice. "Ash!" Stavros called, he was moving towards Ash quickly, almost in a run.

"D-dad?" Ash blinked. What was wrong with him? Did he dream about those people? Ash felt wrong, like his soul just got fucked and slammed against mountains. He heard his father say something but had no idea what he said. He was gasping for breath, clenching his chest as if he was trying to keep his heart from jumping out. His eyes were blurry, was he crying? He was about to reach up to check but his knees suddenly gave out.

"ASH!" Stavros shouted, catching his son before he hit the ground. "Ash?" his heart quickened as worry flooded his entire body. "What happened?" he demanded, looking at Helliana.

"I don't know," she said quickly, mirroring Stavros' worried look. "We were walking and he just froze! It was like he was lost in another world and then he mentioned seeing people but I have no idea who… I.." she trailed off, having no idea what to say.

Ash groaned slightly and felt like he was going to throw up. He realized he was in his dad's arms but he couldn't focus. He only knew Stavros was talking because he felt the vibration in his chest. "Papa" Ash said in a really faint voice. He hadn't called him 'Papa' since he was nine.

"I'm here baby. I got you," Stavros said soothingly. He adjusted his grip on Ash so he could carry him bridal style and quickly headed out to his car, making sure Helliana was following behind him.

Everything around Ash faded, he swore he heard faint screams around him but from what? He heard that deep chuckle again before everything went black.

"He has to stay hidden." a man spoke but Ash had no idea who had said it or where he even was. "Keep him safe, no one can know." that same voice said.

Ash heard soft crying, he looked around and saw a familiar sight before him. It was that same room but it wasn't storming outside this time, he didn't hear screams like before. Ash stood in the middle of the room and as his eyes drifted around he realized the room was empty. No bed, no dresser, no toy chest… nothing. He didn't notice he had left the room until he was in the hallway.

"Please, you can't leave me like this." It was a woman's voice this time, she was clearly crying. "I love you, you promised we'd stick together, remember?" she had sobbed.

There was a brief pause before the male spoke again, "I had promised, and I meant it, when I had loved you."

The woman began to sob at that moment and he heard a heavy sigh before he heard a door slamming shut, the woman began to wail in sorrow. Ash stumbled forward, needing to see what was going on. He rushed to the door and tried pulling it open but somehow, it was stuck.

'You aren't ready to see what's on the other side of that door' Ash heard a voice echoing in his head. He tried to speak but no words came out. He turned towards the sound of crying, tilting his head seeing a pregnant lady kneeling on the floor, crying into her hands. Her blonde, almost white, hair was long, so long it touched the floor. She wore a white gown and her body glowed a faint white.

Ash took a step towards her but froze when the woman suddenly stopped crying and snapped her head up, her piercing blue eyes stared right at him. Could she see him? Wasn't this a dream?

"Wake up, Ash, Wake up!," her scream echoed so loudly around him.

☽ CHAPTER THIRTEEN ☾

Ash jumped straight out of bed, swearing he could still hear that woman's screaming in his ears. What the fuck was going on? He looked around, slowly relaxing seeing he was in his room.

When did he even get home?

"Ashy?" Dakota asked, standing up from the chair they had been sitting in.

Ash grunted when he was suddenly being squeezed to death, "Hey, Kota," he strained to speak. "Can you let go now? Can't breathe!"

"Oh, sorry." Dakota released him and than slapped him over the head, "Fuck boy, you worried your papa so much his hair almost turned gray." Dakota scolded.

Ash rubbed his head and frowned, "What?" he shook his head, trying to remember what happened.

"Ash," Stavros breathed out from the doorway. It was clear he was relieved seeing his son awake. He moved over to him and hugged him so tight, Ash was sure his bones would break. Ash instantly felt more calm, the comfort of his fathers arms around him made him feel like a small child again, crying over a nightmare he had but his father's embrace always scared away those nightmares.

Ash felt his dad trembling and hugged him extra tightly, "I'm okay, dad" he wanted to sound reassuring but he didn't even believe it.

Pulling back, Stavros looked him over slowly, gently cupping his chin to make the boy look up at him, "Don't ever scare me like that again." His voice was stern but his grip gentle.

"I'm sorry, dad," he replied. "I don't even know what happened." it wasn't a full lie, that whole encounter confused the shit out of him.

"Helliana-"

"Is she okay?" Ash cut in.

"Yes," Stavros said. He wrapped an arm around his shoulders and led him out of his room and down to the kitchen.

"I dropped her off at home before bringing you here. Lucky for you, Lucian is here and he checked you over. He suspects you had a panic attack of some sorts." Stavros explained. "You've been asleep for two days," he added. He gestured for Ash to sit at the table while he moved over to the fridge and began pulling things out to get some food into the boy.

"Panic attack," Ash repeated, frowning as he sat down. "I've never had a panic attack before," he could honestly say he never wanted one again.

Stavros got some soup heating up on the stove before buttering up some toast. He poured a cup of orange juice and set that with the toast on the table in front of Ash.

"Eat, you need your strength." Stavros ordered, his tone soft. "Helliana mentioned you saw people, but she had no idea who you were talking about." He said, sitting down.

Ash nibbled at a piece of toast and thought about whether he should get into what he saw or not. What if everyone thought he was crazy? He didn't even know if what he saw was real, let alone how to even describe the sudden rush of fear he felt. Who was that man? Why was he smirking at him like they knew each other?

"She said she didn't see anyone, I guess my eyes were playing tricks on me or something." Ash murmured, still clearly bothered by it all, as he picked his toast apart and ate small bites. He couldn't make himself look anywhere but at his toast right now.

"Can we talk about it later?" Ash asked. "You said I was asleep for two days, but it honestly feels like I didn't get any rest."

Stavros wanted to push the issue, demanding answers to understand what happened, but he held his tongue. Whatever happened clearly still bothered Ash and he wasn't about to make the boy relive it so soon after waking up. He stood to check on the soup, pouring it into a bowl when it was ready. "Eat that and then go relax on the couch, okay?" he said, setting the bowl on the table. "I'm sure Lucian will be thrilled seeing you up and he might want to do a quick check over."

"When did they even get here?" Ash asked, pulling the bowl closer and taking a small spoonful, blowing on it so it didn't burn his mouth.

"We showed up when you were on your little date," Lucian said as he walked into the kitchen. "How ya feeling kid?" he asked, sitting on a chair beside Ash and watching him closely.

Ash gave a weak smile, happy to see him even if he didn't have the energy to show it just yet. "Like I had a panic attack and slept for two days, but the food is helping," he replied. Ash had known Lucian and Dakota for as long as he could remember, they were part of his family even though he didn't see them as much as he'd like.

Lucian snorted softly, "Boy, your daddy about died from a heart attack. When you make him worry, you go all out." he said with a chuckle.

Ash rolled his eyes at that but had a grin, "What can I say? I excel at theater" Ash finished half of the soup before he had to stop eating. He stood to handle the dishes but Dakota, who had joined them not too long after, shooed him away.

"Go sit on the couch. I'll take care of these," Dakota instructed him.

Ash knew better than to argue so he just gave a small nod, turning to head into the living room. "Oh," Dakota called after him, "There are two boxes on the table that you can open." they said. Ash perked up with excitement at that and wasted no time going to see what was in the box.

Lucian looked over at Stavros, who was sitting at the table staring down at his coffee lost in his own thoughts, and cleared his throat. "Stavros?" he asked, arching a brow in surprise seeing the man do a little jump.

Stavros had been so lost in his own thoughts that Lucian's sudden voice startled him. It was worrying, a bit, since nothing startled him.

"Yes?" Stavros replied, forcing himself to look away from his coffee to meet Lucian's gaze. "Are you okay?" he asked, worried for his friend.

With a heavy sigh, Stavros nodded, "No." he said. "That's not important, though."

Lucian knew not to push him on that so, instead, he went to a new topic, "Do you plan on telling Ash about what's been happening?" he asked.

"No," he replied quickly. "He just woke up, he doesn't need that all dumped on him right now," "You can't avoid it for too long," Dakota said, finishing the dishes. "Sooner or later he'll want to see Liam."

"I know," Stavros sighed out. "Just, let him relax for an hour or two and then I'll tell him." "Did they say how long the restrictions are up for?" Lucian asked.

Stavros shook his head, opening his mouth to speak but Ash's excited cheer cut him off.

"No way!" Ash yelled, smiling wide as he tore the box open even more. "No fucking way!" he couldn't believe they got him a new laptop!

Stavros shot a glare at the two before standing, making sure to grab his coffee, and headed into the living room.

Dakota followed with Lucian, both taking a seat while smiling wide at Ash's excitement. Ash ripped open the other box and nearly fainted again at the sight of a new playstation. "Spoiling him rotten," Stavros muttered into his cup before taking a sip.

"Well," Lucian said, glancing at the man, "He did deserve something from that bill list. Poor boy was traumatized."

Ash shot to his feet to give them both a tight hug, "You didn't have to get me these," he said, though he wasn't surprised since they always brought him gifts when they came by.

"Thank you both so much, I can't wait to tell Liam!" he exclaimed, going back to his gifts and wasted no time in setting up his laptop.

Dakota looked over at Stavros, who shook his head at them, but Dakota ignored him, "Yeah, about that, Ashy," they paused for a moment.

Ash stopped what he was doing to look up at the three adults, "Is something wrong with Liam?" he asked, already feeling panic rising inside him.

"No!" Dakota and Lucian both said at the same time.

Stavros shut his eyes, clearly annoyed at the two, "You both suck at this," he hissed, opening his eyes to glare at them both. He shook his head and looked at Ash,

"Nothing is wrong with Liam, Patrick is taking care of him." Stavros said, wanting to calm Ash. "These two morons," he shot a pointing glance at them both, "can't seem to wait to destroy your happiness so I guess we are having this talk now." He gestured for Ash to sit again before he continued speaking.

"There has been an emergency restriction put in place yesterday. Seven more bodies have been found-"

"Where?" Ash interrupted.

Stavros sighed, taking a sip of his coffee and wanting to kill Lucian and Dakota. This conversation easily could have waited, it wasn't like Ash was about to run out the door or anything, but no, let's cause him to panic or be afraid, it's fine. Fucking fine.

"In the east end," he finally replied. "Don't panic," he added, "Liam is safe with Pat."

Ash didn't believe that for a second, something had always felt off about Patrick and Tyler, which made it hard to trust them.

"So with the restrictions, it means no children are allowed to go out at all without an adult and absolutely no one is allowed outside once nightfall." Stavros continued. He studied Ash for a moment, "This is serious, Ash. No. Sneaking. Out." he said each word sharply, wanting to make sure Ash fully understood. "You can call Liam to check on him or you can even ask me to bring you to see him but you can not, I repeat, Can NOT, sneak out, understood?" he asked.

Ash slowly nodded his head, his mind already racing with so many thoughts. Everything was fine a month ago, but ever since Patrick and Tyler showed up, shit hit the fan. He didn't know how they were responsible for it but he just knew it had to be them.

Lucian and Dakota helped Ash bring everything to the game room, they all were chatting about random things as they got everything set up in an attempt to keep Ash distracted, it only sort of worked.

"Do you guys know Patrick and Tyler?" Ash randomly asked, sitting on the couch. They both paused to look at the boy.

"Yes," Dakota said. "Patrick and I were close once but drifted apart when he started acting like an idiot." they said, a heavy sigh leaving them.

"I only met them a few times. I wanted to stab Patrick just for the fact he can't use a fucking oven but the moron can drive a manual?." Lucian said, obviously annoyed by that. "Tyler didn't seem too bad though, maybe a little too polite and stuck up but he was able to handle his brother pretty well."

Dakota laughed lightly, "I know if Patrick was my brother I would have killed him long ago." "Did they feel…. Off to you?" Ash asked.

"Off how?" Lucian questioned.

"I don't know. Everytime I'm around them it just feels," he frowned, trying to think of the right word, "Wrong. I can't explain it. It's like my intuition knows they are bad news somehow." Dakota tilted their head slightly, "I don't get that way around them. It's clear Patrick isn't right in the head, but they seem harmless." they said, shrugging a shoulder.

"I don't know about harmless, but they definitely aren't a threat." Lucian said. He had no idea how to handle this conversation but luckily Ash just seemed to drop it, for now.

After setting up everything in the game room, the three talked for a few hours while playing some games but dinner time came and went pretty quickly. Ash was up in his room later than normal, getting ready for bed because school had been canceled until things calmed down with the murders, which was nice, but also annoying since he couldn't go anywhere without an adult. "Hey," Stavros said, walking into the room after giving a small knock on the doorframe, since the door was open.

Ash put his dirty shirt in the hamper, "Hey," he said, turning to look at him.

"How are you feeling?" his dad asked, sighing when Ash just offered a shrug in response. "You know you can talk to me about anything," he said, sitting on the edge of his bed.

Ash nodded while he also sat on his bed, "I know, I just don't know if what I saw was actually real or not." he said softly.

"Well talk to me about it and we can try figuring it out?" he suggested.

Ash opened his mouth, but closed it for a moment as he tried gathering his thoughts.

"I honestly don't even know what happened. I was walking with Helliana and this chick with gross pink hair walked by," he said, frowning some. "I think she was a nun because I found it so odd that a nun would have pink hair… but she walked by and said 'Nothing is truly what it seems'. I had no idea what she was talking about but I wasn't able to talk and she didn't even stop," Ash explained, glancing at his father, "She kept walking like I wasn't even there and then I felt this..I don't even know." Ash sighed. He rubbed his face, trying to remember it all clearly and think on how to explain it.

"I was suddenly cold and I felt this presence, a strong one, staring at me but I had no idea from where until I saw the pink nun walking towards this…thing. He looked like a man but he had fangs! And claws!" He was still stunned by it all. "He was just staring at me with these glowing red eyes. It was like he was staring right into my soul and sucking it out or something and everything around me just faded away." Ash felt his heart quickening just thinking about that man as he looked down at his hands.

Stavros listened intently, his own anger slowly rising, "Did anything else happen?" he asked curiously.

Ash shook his head, "No, I don't think…." he trailed off. Ash lifted his head to look up at his father, "Yeah, actually, he 'shh" me." he said, holding his finger to his lip to mimic the motion. "He was smirking, lifted a creepy clawed finger to his lips to shh me. I have no idea why and since Helliana said she didn't even see anyone I don't even know if it happened or if my eyes were playing tricks on me." he said. He ran his fingers through his hair, staring at his floor, "It just felt so real and I was completely frozen in my spot. I couldn't bring myself to even breathe or turn away, it's like any movement from me would cause that man, or creature, or whatever he was, to swallow me whole." he whispered, his voice shaking as he spoke.

Stavros swallowed down his anger as he listened to his son's words. He wrapped an arm around his shoulders and pulled him close, "I don't know if it was real or not but I'll keep you safe. Just remember I'm here and nothing can get you." he said, hoping to comfort him. He kissed the top of his head before he stood up, "Now try getting some sleep and forget about that, okay?" he suggested.

Ash gave a weak smile and shifted on his bed to lay down under the covers, "Good night, dad," he said softly.

"Goodnight, son, I love you." Stavros said, turning his light off as he walked out of the room. "Love you too" Ash whispered. He stared at the darkness in his room, suddenly feeling so exposed. Ash growled at himself for his ridiculous thoughts and turned over on his bed to face the wall, not noticing the faint glow of two red eyes staring at him from the far corner.

☽ CHAPTER FOURTEEN ☾

"What the fuck do you think you are doing!" Stavros shouted into his phone. He was angrily pacing in his office, his eyes narrowed as he listened to laughter on the other end. "Whatever do you mean?" a man laughed out innocently. "I have been cooped up at home plucking feathers from a little birdie."

"Don't play games with me, you fucking piece of shit" Stavros snarled.

A sudden loud shriek came from the other end, causing Stavros to pull the phone from his ear just slightly, "What the fuck are you doing? Pay attention to me!" he bellowed.

"Needy, needy," the man laughed. "I already informed you I was busy." his voice came out in a taunt. "Though I do enjoy the fun foreplay of being degraded, I can't talk long so what do you want?"

"I know you were at the mall" Stavros snapped, completely ignoring his foreplay comment. "When?" the man asked.

"Don't play fucking dumb with me, two days ago!"

"Are you sure? I'd think I'd remember something like that… wait, which mall?" the man asked, his voice filled with amusement, another shriek sounding in the background.

Stavros gripped his phone so tightly he was surprised it didn't shatter. "I swear to the fucking Gods-"

"You really shouldn't swear, it's not polite." the voice cut in. "Besides, don't gods smite people for doing something so stupid?"

Stavros let out a very heavy sigh, stopping in his tracks to get himself under control, "I know you were talking to my son."

"Your son?" There was a short pause, "I didn't know you had a son." "Stop playing fucking games!" Stavros shouted.

"Calm down, no need to shout." the male laughed. "How do you know it was me?" "Because I don't know anyone else who has a crazy fucking pink-haired nun by his side!" Stavros snapped.

"Oh, that's rude, she isn't that crazy." another shriek filled the air. "Yea, I guess that was me. Weird, figured that'd be something I'd remember."

"Stay the fuck away from my son or I swear I will kill you." Stavros hissed through his teeth. "You know," the man said, completely ignoring the threat, "I was just trying to keep him well informed. The world is so dangerous these days and as his uncle, I just wanted to help."

"You are not part of his family. Leave. Him. Alone." Stavros growled, slamming his phone on his desk after hanging up.

☽ CHAPTER FIFTEEN ☾

It had been five days since Tyler returned home with Dan, it was rocky at first but things seemed to be going rather okay, so far. Tyler stuck around and helped his father cope with no alcohol and Dan, even though he had moments of rage, overall he seemed to be slowly getting better.

Liam had kept the secret that his father was home even though it was hard. He wanted to tell Ash about how it was going, that his father was home now and was starting to act like a father, but Patrick kept insisting that Liam remain quiet about it.

It was a week before the school dance and Ash still wasn't getting the hang of how to do anything.

"Why do I even have to learn to dance?" Ash grumbled. They had moved things around in the living room so they had an open floor and could dance without bumping into things.

Stavros sighed, "Because you are taking a lady to a dance."

"Yeah but kids these days don't actually dance. They just stand around talking and laughing." Ash said.

Stavros rolled his eyes as he sat on the couch to take a break. "You are getting better at this. You just have to stop being so tense and stop stepping on my feet."

"You have huge feet. If they were a normal size I wouldn't step on them so much. Helliana has normal feet. I'm not at risk of stepping on them."

Liam laughed, "Might want to warn her to wear steel toe shoes."

Ash glared over at him as he crossed his arms over his chest. "Haha. Very funny." "Shall we try this again?" Stavros asked. He stood up and held out his hand to Ash.

Ash groaned but took his father's hand and put his left hand on Stavros' waist. He was trying to learn how to lead the dance this time. He muttered to himself and stepped forward but ended up stepping on Stavros' toe and tripping over him. Stavros was quick to catch Ash before his face planted on the floor.

"You guys aren't even listening to the right music. I'd just like to point out that kids these days don't really do the waltz or any of that stuff. They pretty much just grind against each other." Liam said with a chuckle.

Stavros released Ash and stepped back from him, "I'm not teaching you that and you better not be grinding against her." His eyes slowly narrowed as he spoke. "I'll be there and watching so make sure there is space between you two."

"This is all your fault, Liam. Had you just left it all alone I wouldn't be in this mess right now." Liam laughed at Ash's words, "True. You'd be pouting because you would be staying home and not going to the dance with the girl you really like."

Ash opened his mouth to speak but was silenced when Liam's cell rang. Liam pulled his cell from his jeans pocket and answered.

"I won't be grinding against her, dad." Ash said, turning his attention to his father. "If she wants to dance I'll dance with her but she won't be mad if we end up just standing on the side and talking instead."

Stavros shook his head slowly, "Schools shouldn't do a dance if no one dances at it. What's the point?"

Ash shrugged, "None of the kids seem to complain about it so why bother stopping?"

"I have to go." Liam said. He walked to the front door and pulled on his boots and his coat. There wasn't a whole lot of snow on the ground, maybe an inch or two, but Liam got cold so easily and he knew his toes would freeze off if he didn't wear winter boots.

"Something wrong?" Ash asked.

Liam shook his head, "No, I just need to get home. I'll see you in school tomorrow." he said. He waved bye and quickly ran out of the house before any more questions were asked. His father was the one who called him and Liam had no idea what was going on but he was worried. His father was yelling about something and right now Tyler was getting groceries and Patrick had left a day ago to take care of some other business. His father didn't sound drunk so maybe something was actually wrong? It had always been hard to understand his father when he yelled because he'd jump all over the place with his words and be calm for a few seconds before going back into a raging fit.

"Dad?" Liam called out, walking into the house tapped the toe of his boots to knock the snow off before removing his coat and shoes. He looked around the house, it seemed quiet right now he walked towards the living room but stopped hearing something behind him. He turned and let out a startled cry when something hard collided with his stomach. He fell onto his knees gasping for air as he held his stomach, his mouth watered as drool dripped from his lips. The pain was enough to bring all too familiar tears and stars to his eye. Looking up at his father's angry face staring down at him, Liam realized his father reeked of whiskey. Fear creeped up the boy's spine for he knew this was about to get so much worse when his father's left arm listed into the air with a belt clenched around his fist. "Dad, I'm sorry!".

☽ CHAPTER SIXTEEN ☾

Helliana hesitantly walked up to Ash's front door and knocked on it. She had been worried about him since he passed out at the mall and she hadn't heard anything about him since. She shivered as a cold breeze passed by and smiled when Stavros opened the door with a tilt of his head.

"Hello, Helliana, come in out of that cold." he said, opening the door wider as he stepped back. "Thank you, Mr. Morana." She said sweetly. She stepped inside and glanced around.

"What brings you here?" Stavros asked, shutting the door.

Helliana looked up at him, unable to believe how tall the man was, "I was hoping to see Ash. I haven't seen him since the mall and I was getting worried." she admitted.

Stavros walked towards the stairs, "I'll go get him for you." he said. He headed upstairs and knocked on Ash's door.

Lucian and Dakota were still there, being nosy and poking their heads out from the kitchen just to catch a glimpse of the lady who caught Ash's eye.

Ash opened his door, "Hey dad, what's up?" he asked.

Stavros leaned against the doorframe while crossing his arms, smirking, "Oh nothing, just a concerned little lady at the door wanting to check on your health." he teased.

Ash went wide eyed, "Helliana's here?" he asked. He quickly straightened out his clothes and looked to his dad for reassurance, "Do I look okay?" he asked, though he didn't even wait for a response. He was surprised she came to see him but he was also happy about it. Letting out a sharp breath of courage, he slipped past his father and headed downstairs, instantly smiling seeing her.

"Hey, Helliana." he said, reaching the bottom step.

"Hey," she replied. "I just wanted to see how you were doing."

"I'm doing good." he said, feeling awkward because he could tell his father was at the top of the steps just staring at them.

"Would you like to come in? We can hang out in the game room?" Ash suggested.

Helliana gave a small shake of her head, "I can't stay horribly long. My mom is waiting for me in the car but I haven't seen you in school or got any updates about you."

"Oh, I'm sorry, I didn't know no one told you anything." Ash said softly. "I was resting for two days, I only woke up yesterday afternoon," he explained. "I wanted to go to school today but-" "With all the murders they don't have classes on Friday anymore." Helliana cut in. "I hope they find out who's doing it soon. I heard a rumor that if anymore happen they'll be canceling school all together and even the dance." she said. She prayed they found out who did it, she couldn't believe someone was going around killing people and so far it seemed like it was for no reason. "I am happy you are doing better, did you see the doctors? Do they know what happened?" Helliian asked, wanting to change the topic.

Ash sat on the bottom step while shaking his head, "I had a panic attack." he said. "My Uncle Lucian is here so he checked me over."

Helliana tilted her head slightly, "A panic attack? Was it because of those two people you saw?" she asked.

Ash flinched at the reminder and gave a nod, "Yeah, I don't even know if they were real. I think my eyes were just playing tricks on me." he said.

Helliana glanced back at the door hearing a honk and sighed heavily, "That's my mom." she said. She looked back at Ash, giving him a sweet smile, "It's good seeing you and I hope I'll see you for the dance." she said.

"It's great seeing you too!" Ash said, jumping to his feet. He didn't want her to go but he knew it was best.

"Oh, here," Helliana pulled out a piece of paper and held it out to him, "It's my cell number so you can text me next time you pass out to let me know you're okay" she giggled softly.

Ash blushed brightly as he stepped forward and took the piece of paper. His fingers brushed against hers and sent a shiver through him. God, her skin was so soft and perfect that he was just tempted to caress her everywhere. Ash quickly cleared that thought from his head as she walked out the door and was smiling so wide that his mouth was starting to hurt.

Ash heard someone behind him clear their throat and slowly turned to see his father, Lucian, and Dakota standing behind him. He didn't even know when they got there and he cursed at how silent they moved.

"If I catch you up at 3am talking to her, or doing some kind of nasty messaging with her, I'm taking that phone of yours away." Stavros warned.

"Oh don't be mean, Stabby. My little angel would never do such a thing." Dakota cooed, going over to Ash and hugging him close, "Don't worry Ashy, I'll protect you from big meanie daddy." They laughed.

"I don't know about that, Dakota, it's pretty easy for a woman to turn a 'little angel' into a big demon." Lucian said, grinning and glancing over at Stavros.

Stavros reached up to rub his temples while sighing heavily, "I need coffee."

Ash rolled his eyes as he pulled away from Dakota, "Yeah, yeah." he chuckled. He slipped the paper into his pocket and grinned, "you two want to play a game?" he asked.

Lucian shrugged, "I'm down." he said.

Dakota nodded, "That sounds lovely. You two go get things set up and I'll make some popcorn for us." they said.

Stavros shook his head, "So nice of you to ask," he said, playfully glaring at them, "I'll just do boring work in my office."

Ash snorted, "You never want to play video games."

"Probably because he always loses," Dakota laughed, walking to the kitchen. Stavros scoffed, "I don't always lose."

"Well then let's go, I'm always ready to beat you again" Ash said, laughing as he ran to the game room.

Stavros quickly followed him, only pausing to give Lucian a slight glare, "You are getting a little too comfortable with what you say." were his only words before walking into the game room.

Lucian rolled his eyes at that but just followed behind.

☽ CHAPTER SEVENTEEN ☾

"I want him to die," Liam whispered. He had given up on believing his father would get sober and be a real dad to him. He was curled up in the bathroom, new bruises covered his arms, back, and stomach. He rubbed his eyes and shivered a little before he gasped out, nearly jumped out of his skin when he looked up and suddenly Patrick was sitting there on the side of the bathtub. "How the hell did you get here?" Liam demanded.

"You called me." Patrick replied, a small grin on his face. "So I came."

Liam narrowed his eyes "I never called you." He quickly stood up and grabbed the bathroom door handle and turned it but Patrick was up and keeping the door shut with his hand in an instant.

"You did call me. Your sorrow called out and I answered. I feel your pain, know your rage, I'm here to make your desire come true." he purred softly, his face inches away from Liam's.

Liam felt his breath catch in his throat and he wanted to scream, he felt panicked, but the way Patrick was staring at him was almost calming, in a way. He watched those eyes go from the

normal hazel to a flash of yellow, then returning to the normal eye color. "What are you?" Liam heard himself whisper out. He wasn't sure he'd want the answer.

Patrick smirked darkly and stepped closer to Liam. He ran his fingertips over Liam's cheek slowly "I'm a demon" he purred. "I'm here for you, to help you get your dark desires." he whispered. "I'll take away those that cause you great pain." he purred, an evil grin on his lips. Liam stumbled back away from the door, his face holding the look of horror and his breath catching in his throat once again as his back hit the door. He just stared, unable to find his voice as a thousand thoughts ran through his mind. Was it seriously true? Maybe some kind of sick joke? "You're lying" he heard himself whisper out. No way this was actually true.

Patrick tilted his head slowly and held back a chuckle "Lying? Why would I lie to you?" he asked. "I get to fill out your dark desires, you can't hide them from me. I know what they are. I know who you want revenge against, I know you want to make those suffer the way they made you suffer." he purred. "You will not act on them yourself, so I get to do the dirty work."

"For what? my soul." Liam growled out. "Why would I agree to shit like that? What makes you think I'd want that?" Liam hissed.

Patrick grinned and watched him for a moment, his eyes flashing the sickening yellow, as if peering into Liam's soul. "You may not agree to it now but in the end someone always becomes desperate enough to take on the deal. A soul is worthless to you, it's filled with sorrow, fear, hate, and pain, and yet those are the sweet flavors that one, such as myself, craves." he licked his lips at the thought of tasting his delicious soul.

"Oh so I get sweet revenge but then get to burn in hell? Sounds like some sweet messed up deal" Liam rolled his eyes. He couldn't believe this was actually a conversation he was having. Maybe he was having a horrible dream? There was just no way this was real.

Patrick laughed softly and shook his head "Who ever said you'd burn in hell?" he smirked. "Your father is not going to change. You are a punching bag to him just like you are to your mother.

You will be beaten and tormented by them everyday until you are pushed to do the unthinkable. A human soul can only take so much until it finally snaps and that raises the question on how much you believe you are capable of taking before you finally snap?"

Liam swallowed roughly "I'm strong enough to take it.." he whispered. He didn't believe his own words and it showed.

"For how long? Months? Years? You'll reach your moment of breaking and do the unthinkable and waste such a perfect soul" Patrick replied smoothly.

Liam looked away, his breathing felt heavy to him "What is unthinkable?" he whispered, though he knew he already knew the answer to that question.

"Such a silly question to ask." Patrick said. He moved over to Liam and gently grabbed the boys chin to make him look up into his eyes "Every soul gets to a horrible point in its life, some are strong enough to push past it but others give up all hope and when that happens they decide death is a lot more welcoming than life is and so they end it." he replied.

Liam's eyes widened as he stared into the demon's eyes. He felt a scream catch in his throat, terror filled him and he quickly had to push the demon out of his way to throw up in the toilet. He gagged and spit, trying to regain control of himself to stop from throwing up again. "You're lying" he gasped out, spitting in the toilet.

Liam heard the demon chuckle behind him "As I have said, I have no need to lie. What you saw is true. Think of my offer, I can be of great service to you and when you decide to use me simply call out my name." The demon whispered beside Liam's ear before he simply vanished in yellow smoke.

Liam clung to the toilet, as if holding onto it for dear life. He couldn't forget what he saw, couldn't even find the words to speak of what he saw. He didn't want to believe it but in those eyes he saw it and part of him knew it would become true. In those sickening yellow eyes he saw himself, body limp on the ground, foam all over his mouth, eyes wide open and lifeless with an empty pill bottle beside him. Liam swallowed hard and stood on shaky legs, he turned on the water and washed his face before he looked in the mirror and stumbled back with a small sob escaping him. He saw his lifeless body in the mirror and he knew it had to be true. He saw his own death caused by his own hand.

Liam stumbled from his bathroom and into his room. He couldn't sleep, the hours of night ticked by but he couldn't even shut his eyes for a minute. He couldn't stop trembling, couldn't stop crying. He kept seeing his dead body over and over again, how had Patrick shown him that?

What if it wasn't true? What if the demon was just trying to get his soul? Why did a demon even need a soul? He had so many questions running around his head but he had no answers. He stayed on his bed, holding his knees tightly to his chest and stared at the floor as his mind went in a whirlpool of thoughts.

"You should have waited longer before telling him the truth." Tyler said, standing beside Patrick. The two men stood on a rooftop across the street from Liam's house. It was nearing 2 am so it was still pretty dark out.

Patrick put his hands in his jeans pockets and shrugged lightly "I could have." he smirked. "But his emotions are already high up there. He's almost perfect to feed from, soon I'll have his mind snapping with insanity." he licked his lips. He couldn't wait to devour such a tortured soul.

Tyler raised a brow and glanced at him sideways "Take care, brother. You push things too fast with him and it won't be as you want it. Snap him too much and he'll no longer be your dinner." "Oh shut up." Patrick hissed. "You get the father, why are you bitching about this? You've already twisted Dan's mind. I would have thought you would have collected him by now."

Tyler smirked "Oh don't worry, I'll be tasting his blackened soul soon enough. We just need to confirm it's allowed, since, you know, those assholes like to change their minds at the last second."

"I never knew you as someone who actually waited for such things. What is it everyone always says? Better to ask for forgiveness than permission?" Patrick chuckled. "Wait, don't tell me, little baby is scared" he fake pouted.

Tyler rolled his eyes and shoved him "That is how the saying goes, however, for the one we would ask for forgiveness from, it's highly unlikely he would give it. Everyone knows he doesn't like others feeding on his land, I don't blame him. He has juicy souls here, it just happens to be our luck that the emotions running through Liam and Dan are not to his taste." he pointed out. "Besides, we'll get our answer tomorrow. Until then, we wait."

"I hate waiting," Patrick groaned. "It's like having to wait for foreplay to end in sex. Why men bother to waste time on such a useless thing is beyond me. Who cares if the chick enjoys it? Personally, I hate foreplay, as long as I enjoy myself and reach the end I don't care how she feels about it."

"It always amazes me how we go from talking about souls, to you mentioning something about sex. Damn, by now I have a clear image in my mind how you do sex from all the crap you mention. I know, foreplay is beyond you, but have you ever thought that maybe, just maybe, it might be more enjoyable if you actually knew what you were doing?" Tyler said with a sigh. Oh he was getting a headache now, he really wished Patrick was quiet but sadly he was never that lucky.

"What? are you offering to teach me such skills? Oh great master?" Patrick joked and smirked. Tyler narrowed his eyes "Am I the only one who knows we are brothers? Has that information slipped your mind?" he growled in disgust.

Patrick smirked as he shrugged "What? We share souls sometimes, is sharing a woman really that different?"

Tyler shuddered "Oh you are sick. Yes, dumbass, sharing a soul is so far different than sharing a woman. I don't have to see your naked ass, for one, and they are both filling in their own ways."

"I thought you did the filing with a female?" Patrick was enjoying himself.

"I need to bleach my ears out." Tyler shuddered again. "I know you like to do sick jokes but please, for me, leave me out of them for now on so I don't die from vomiting." he groaned. He rubbed his temples and stepped back from Patrick "I can't believe you are my brother… you act like a damned child."

Patrick rose a brow "How many children do you know-"

"I take that back!" Tyler cut in. "I don't need to know what you were about to say. I'm sure it was far from pleasant. I'm going to the hotel to wait for an answer. You do as you please, just… do it far from me." Tyler turned and walked off. He knew by now he really shouldn't be surprised by all the crazy crap his brother said, but he still got shocked by some things.

Patrick chuckled under his breath as he glanced back and watched as Tyler faded away. He rolled his eyes, "Big baby." Patrick crouched down as he watched the house, he couldn't see what Liam was doing but he could feel everything happening to him. "Soon, little pet, you'll be ready." he purred. He licked his lips and turned as he stood to walk off. He knew his brother was right, they couldn't feast until they got the OK but at this point, whether he got the ok or not, he was going to enjoy that boy's soul.

☽ CHAPTER EIGHTEEN ☾

Liam trembled as he walked to Ash's house, lost in thought trying to wrap his mind over what had happened with Patrick. He hadn't seen the demon since last night but he was grateful for that. Demon. He still couldn't believe it. Were demons even real? Well, clearly, since Patrick was one. Did that mean Tyler was one too? They were brothers… he honestly couldn't see just one of them being a demon. He didn't bother knocking as he walked into Ash's house, barely noticed he removed his boots or coat before heading up to Ash's room. He opened the door and frowned, not seeing Ash there. He headed down to the game room and let out a defeated sigh not seeing him there either.

"Liam?" Stavros asked, sitting at the kitchen table drinking coffee and looking over some papers. Liam actually jumped at Stavros' voice and turned slowly before he headed into the kitchen. "Ash around?" he asked softly. He rubbed his arm nervously, his body aching from the beating he got from his father but he wasn't going to breathe a word of that to Stavros.

"No, sorry, he went out with Lucian and Dakota about an hour ago." Stavros replied. He knew something was wrong with the boy, he looked pale and was jumpy but he didn't understand why. "How are things going? Your father still doing okay at the center?" he asked.

Liam held back a whimper at the thought of his father and forced himself to smile, wishing Ash was here right now.

"He's doing okay. Tyler said his anger got a little out of control but he's fine." Liam said, a little too quickly. "Can you tell Ash I stopped by?" he asked.

Stavros frowned, knowing the boy was lying but decided not to push the issue, "You are more than welcome to wait here for him. He shouldn't be out too much longer" he replied. "I can-" "No!" Liam snapped, flinching at his own sharp tone. "No, thank you," he said, making sure his voice was calmer. "Patrick is by himself and I don't want to risk him burning the place down." he forced a chuckle. He headed to the front door quickly, yanking on his coat and boots once he got there.

Stavros stood and followed him, "Are you okay?" he asked.

Liam nodded, "Of course." he smiled. "Just tired and feeling a little sick but that's probably from the cold weather," he said. He pulled open the door and stepped outside, pausing when Stavros spoke.

"You can talk to me, you know. I'm not sure what struggles you are going through currently but I am here and I can help you." he said softly.

Liam just gave a nod and started walking again, only to stop once more when Stavros grabbed his arm gently.

"It's getting late, Liam, and you shouldn't be out by yourself. It's dangerous." he said.

"I'll be fine," Liam said, pulling his arm away and wincing ever so slightly at the pain it caused. Stavros didn't believe him for a second, "Let me drive you home." he said, his voice leaving little room for argument.

Liam wanted to tell the man to piss off but Stavros had always been there for him and he couldn't bring himself to be outright rude like that.

"Okay," he whispered.

Stavros wasted no time grabbing his keys and slipping his boots on, knowing the others would be gone long enough for him to drop Liam off. He shut the door as he left the house heading straight to the car, glancing at Liam to make sure he followed.

Once they both got in, Stavros took off towards his house.

The ride felt like it lasted forever to Liam, especially since neither one spoke a word but he was thankful for that. He couldn't wrap his mind around anything right now, no way would he be able to actually explain it in a conversation. Besides, what would he even say? 'Hey, you know Patrick and Tyler right? Well, they are demons, so, could you possibly kick them out of my house? Oh! And my father is back and beat the shit out of me.' yea, that would go over well.

Stavros glanced around outside as he drove, the town seemed abandoned now that everyone was afraid to go outside but who could blame them? It was clear the murders weren't linked to drug dealers so that left a lot more questions unanswered and the fear was so high, Stavros could almost smell it in the air.

It didn't take too long until he was pulling up to Liam's house, he parked the car and unbuckled his seat belt, however Liam was already out of the car.

"Thanks for the ride!" Liam called out, having shut the door and practically ran into his house. He didn't feel safe at home but where could he go? His mother wouldn't want him there and, currently, he didn't feel comfortable being alone with Stavros. The man was scary and wouldn't take long before he realized something was horribly wrong.

Liam wasn't sure if it was his father, Tyler, or Patrick doing something in the kitchen but he knew someone was in there because he heard dishes banging together and water running. Without a word, he went straight to his room as quietly as possible, hoping he could just be forgotten for a few hours.

Ash was laughing as he walked into the door with Lucian and Dakota. He removed his jacket and boots while shaking his head, "That's not true." he said, chuckling.

Dakota, who stepped to the side after removing their own items, smirked, "It is true." "What's true?" Stavros asked, having gotten back not too long ago and was brewing himself fresh coffee.

"You got banned from a coffee shop because you stole their whole coffee supply?" Ash asked, already laughing again.

Stavros shut his eyes and groaned, "Why am I not surprised you'd tell him that." "It's true?!" Ash exclaimed, laughing.

"Okay, no, I mean, yes, kind of. I didn't steal their whole supply, I just stole a few bags, but they didn't even need all of it."

"You grounded me for breaking into an asylum but stealing coffee is okay?" Ash laughed. Stavros sighed heavily, "Yeah, well, I got my ass beat by my father for doing it and I got banned so I didn't go unpunished."

Ash kept laughing, unable to believe his father would actually steal something but not surprised that he stole coffee.

Stavros shook his head, "Isn't it time you two went home?" he grumbled, glaring at Dakota and Lucian.

"You haven't fully suffered, so, no." Lucian said, grinning.

"Anyways," Stavros said quickly, looking to Ash, "Liam stopped by a short while ago looking for you. He seemed troubled by something but he wouldn't talk to me." he said, shrugging his shoulders.

"He didn't stay?" Ash asked, sobering and frowning.

"No," Stavros said, shaking his head, "He seemed adamant to go home once he discovered you weren't home." he said. "I dropped him off so he would get home safely."

Ash nodded and pulled out his phone, quickly dialing Liam's number and heading up to his room while it rang. When he got Liam's voicemail, he frowned, redialing the number but, again, it went to voicemail. He sent him a text, starting to become a bit worried since Liam normally answered him but even his text went unanswered. He sighed, figuring maybe he went to bed early, so he decided he'd talk to him in school tomorrow. Ash took a shower and got himself ready for bed, making sure to wish everyone a goodnight and checking his phone once more for any word from Liam.

☽ CHAPTER NINETEEN ☾

Ash had been trying to reach Liam for two days. He hadn't seen him at school, at first he thought he was sick, even when he'd try to text or call him, he heard nothing back. He stopped by after school on Monday but no one answered the door. He was starting to get really worried, it wasn't like Liam to miss days of school without at least texting to complain about being sick or whatever was going on.

Ash rubbed the back of his neck as he walked into his house and kicked off his shoes. He tossed his backpack on the ground and glanced at his phone once more. Nothing. "Where are you Liam?" he whispered. He rubbed his forehead as he walked to the kitchen to get himself a glass of orange juice.

"Is something wrong?" Stavros asked, leaning against the doorframe by the hall.

"Jesus!" Ash jumped, sighing as he spilt some juice all over the counter. "Damn dad, don't sneak up on me like that."

Stavros chuckled, "A little jumpy, are we?" he asked. "Don't tell me you did something stupid that will end up with you getting into trouble?" he asked, thinking that might be why he was jumpy. Though, the thought of his nightmares coming back would explain it too, he used to get them a lot as a child.

Ash cleaned up the juice and tossed the cloth into the sink "No." he said, his voice full of worry. "It's Liam… he hasn't been at school at all this week and he isn't answering his phone… I'm just worried. It's not like him." he murmured.

Stavros frowned as he crossed his arms over his chest "How long has it been since you last heard from him?" he asked curiously.

"Um…" Ash rubbed the back of his neck as he thought about it. "We are on Tuesday? I think Friday was the last I talked to him.." he said. Ash turned to look at his dad, "You saw him on Sunday, right?" he asked, "How did he seem?" he asked when his father nodded.

"He seemed bothered by something, but like I said, he wouldn't talk to me." Stavros said.

"This isn't like him.." Ash murmured, mostly to himself. "He always calls me back," he said softly. Stavros growled quietly, not thrilled over the fact that Liam was making Ash worry so much but currently, he wasn't sure what to do about that. He narrowed his eyes for a second, deep in his own thoughts, before he sighed "I'll call his mother and see if she's heard anything from him.." he said.

"Even if he is with his mom, he still would have at least sent a text. He's my best friend, we haven't gone a day without talking since we were like… seven. The only time we don't talk is if we're grounded." Ash replied.

Stavros pushed off the doorframe to take a seat at the table. "Well maybe he got grounded."

"Grounded from school too?" Ash asked. "Highly unlikely. That's like you grounding me and not letting me go to school."

There was something wrong, Ash knew it. He knew there was no way he'd be missing school if he was just grounded, plus, even with his father being off the booze, grounding wasn't a punishment the man used.

"He could have gone to see his father."

Ash shook his head, "He still would have sent me a text."

"You're right." Stavros sighed. "I'll make some calls while you start on homework." He stood up from the table and walked to his office. He shut the door and growled under his breath. Stavros walked to his desk and picked up his phone, he already knew who he had to call.

"You can't stay locked in your room all the damn time! Damnit, boy, don't make me break the fucking door down." Dan yelled from the bottom of the stairs. Tyler was sitting on the couch in the living room just watching as Dan stumbled a bit as he walked, sipping his glass of scotch. "What a troublemaker, isn't he?." Tyler tsked, . He set his drink down on the coffee table while licking his lips. "He's already missed two days of school. What if he misses more?"

"I'll beat his ass black and blue if he does." Dan snapped. He paced the living room and shoved his hands in his pockets "What the hell is wrong with him? He ain't dead." he growled.

Tyler felt his phone vibrate in his pants pocket but he ignored it. He stood up slowly and watched the man continue to pace,"He hasn't done any of his chores either, those dishes are piling up pretty high." Tyler said, a slow smirk forming on his lips. "I think he's just showing so much disrespect towards you." he said, shaking his head, "Man, I'd flip shit if my child acted this way towards me. What do you think he's doing up there?" he asked.

"I don't want to leave my room." Liam whispered, staring at the wall and wishing he was somewhere else. He had hardly moved from his bed ever since Stavros dropped him off.

"You can't stay in bed all day, what if your dad comes storming in here?" Patrick asked softly. He sat at the foot of the bed just watching the boy. He could feel the sorrow and pain coming from him, knowing Liam felt so alone right now while being so full of fear. "You don't need to fear me, Liam."

"You're a demon. What's not to fear? Are you going to be giving me chocolate and pop?" he asked, his eyes shifting down to partly glare at him. "Or a car? No. I doubt that. You only want my soul" Liam whispered, wanting to be far away from him but weirdly enough, also finding some form of comfort with Pat being there. He looked away from him, slowly sat up and swallowed roughly "Why do you even want it?" he asked, glaring at the floor as if it had offended him since he was unable to look at Patrick for too long.

Patrick smirked at his words, "I could give you many things however with your state of mind, having you drive a car is a very bad idea." He said, attempting to lighten the mood a little, " A body can live without a soul, it's not like you'll be dead without one, you'll just be… " he paused as he thought of the right word to use. "Empty, in a way. Taking your soul would be painless and, honestly, you won't even miss it." he purred.

Liam frowned at that, "Empty.." he whispered. How would that feel? Would he really care? Or would he not even notice?. "You haven't answered why you want it," his eyes finally drifted to look over at him.

Patrick grinned while licking his lips "A demon's gotta eat. You'll be dead in a few years anyways, why care what happens to your soul?" he asked.

Liam shuddered at that thought, how did a demon even eat a soul? "What will happen if I die without a soul?" He wasn't sure if he really wanted an answer to that question.

Patrick sighed, already annoyed with the questions, he always got annoyed with the questions. Why did people get so worried about their souls? The only use they seemed to have was feeding a demon. "Nothing happens. You just die. Even with a soul, when you die. You're dead. I don't know if people are teaching that heaven and hell crap, or if they now have new names for them but either way, nothing happens." He paused, looking at Liam and wondered if these answers brought him comfort of some sort, though he doubted it. "There is no bright light at the end of the tunnel, no angels calling out to you, no reaper leading you to the other side." Patrick enjoyed being a demon, he enjoyed all the lies he got to say but he wouldn't start telling the truth now.

"You can't keep pacing back and forth and bitching about everything." Tyler sighed, annoyed with listening to Dan's muttering. "You are making me feel sick. Instead, why not stop pacing and have a few more drinks?" He suggested, holding out the bottle to him with a grin, "Or better yet, grab that belt and beat some sense into your annoying child. It's not like he's willing to leave his room." Tyler smirked, Oh this was always his favorite part. Most demons worked alone, but him and Patrick, well they didn't fight for the same food. Tyler liked his bitter, Patrick enjoyed his doused in sorrow. It's why it worked so well with him, they both knew how to push the right buttons to make their food snap.

Dan curled his lip as he snarled "Fucking child. If he won't come out on his own, I'll drag his ass out." he spat. He jerked the bottle out of Tyler's hand and finished it, throwing it to the side once done and stormed up the stairs after he grabbed his belt. He didn't bother to knock on the door, he kicked it hard, the lock giving out from the force and slamming into the wall.

Liam wiped his eyes, not knowing when exactly he started crying but he didn't care, he looked at Patrick, "Can you really help me?" he asked, his voice soft and filled with defeat.

"Of course," he confirmed.

"Against everyone? My dad, my mom…"

Patrick smirked as he stood up slowly. "I am a demon. There isn't much I can't help you with." he purred.

Liam opened his mouth to speak but ended up jumping when his door was kicked in. He went wide eyed as he watched his dad march into his room and let out a cry when the belt struck his side. He heard his father screaming about something, felt more of the hits, but it all faded as he looked up at Patrick.

Let me help you, Liam. You can't do it on your own.

Patrick's voice spoke in Liam's head, he couldn't speak, couldn't breathe. He knew his father was still hitting him, he felt the painful blows rain down on his body. He heard him continue to yell but it felt like everything slowed down. He watched Patrick, trying to decide if getting his help was the right choice. Who else would help him? Sure, he could talk to Stavros and get his help but what good would come from that? He'd end up in the system or shipped off far away. Patrick rose a brow as he kept his eyes on Liam. He didn't move to stop Dan, he didn't care to. The more the boy got hit and yelled out, the better his soul would taste. Besides, he needed Liam to ask for his help, needed him to know that no one else would be helping him. Patrick smirked darkly, his eyes glowing yellow, when Liam finally gave him a nod. "Oh goody" he purred. "Tyler" he sang out.

Tyler flashed into the room, appearing right behind Dan with a dark chuckle escaping him. The room darkened ever so slightly as Tyler's brown eyes turned white. His fangs grew larger and he caught Dan's arm before he landed another blow on the little pest on the bed. He didn't care about Liam at all, he just wanted his meal.

Dan turned to look at whoever grabbed his arm, blinking in surprise seeing Tyler behind him and went wide eyed seeing his eyes and fangs. Just as he opened his mouth to speak, to demand answers, Tyler yanked him close and sank his fangs into the male's shoulder. He shivered with delight as he fought, Tyler loved when they fought. Dan's blood filled his mouth and tasted

oh-so-sweet, a deep chuckle sounded from his throat as he ripped away from the male's shoulder, tearing the flesh and splattering his blood. Tyler licked his lips, savoring the taste, "Oh so tasty" he purred. He released his grip on Dan, watching him crumble to the floor, gasping and groaning from pain. Tyler wasn't done with him yet, he crouched down in front of Dan and grabbed his chin, forcing the male to look into his eyes, "So twisted. So bitter." he grinned.

Tyler's claws grew and he plunged them deep into his chest, he used his demon strength to punch through his ribs so he could grab the man's heart and slowly started to squeeze. Tyler shut his eyes as he felt the panic soar through the disgusting human, felt his fear, felt the heart beat's slowing. He yanked his hand free, taking the heart out at the same time, and looked down at Dan. He smirked as he stood, crushing the heart in his hand until it turned into ashes and leaving Tyler's hand glowing a faint black. Tyler brought his hand up to his lips and licked his hand slowly, devouring the blackened soul. "Such lovely taste. I'll be full for a long time." he laughed, staring at Dan's lifeless body. He looked over at Liam, unable to hold back another laugh at the look on the boy's face.

Liam stared in horror, unable to believe what he just saw, unable to believe that just happened. He couldn't speak, couldn't scream, or think straight. He was frozen on the floor, not even two feet away from his father's dead body, having no idea what horrified him most. His father's dead body, the demon covered in blood and what he had just done, or the fact he was actually happy he was free.

Patrick shivered in delight, always pleased with bloody kills and enjoyed watching as the light left someone's eye. He moved over to Liam, crouching down to lightly stroke the boy's hair, "Don't worry, my pet. He won't hurt you anymore. No one will." he purred, knowing he got this boy wrapped around his finger. "We can't stay here, little pet," He said, standing up and holding his hand out to the boy. He was close to yanking Liam up to his feet, getting impatient with his frozen state. Then, ever so slowly, Liam turned his attention away from his father to look up at Patrick. Without a word, he reached up to take his hand and slowly stood up, staying close to Patrick in fear of Tyler killing him next. Patrick wrapped an arm around Liam's shoulders and looked at Tyler. "I'll see you in a while." he said, smirking. He knew Tyler enjoyed playing with blood and was no were near done with the body, but Liam didn't need to be here to see how violent Tyler could truly be. Patrick didn't wait for Tyler to speak, he just flashed himself and Liam out of the house to leave Tyler alone.

Stavros cursed as he dropped his cell onto his desk, having tried to call a few times now with no answer, and rubbed his temples. He growled, annoyed that they dare not answer his call, especially since they knew better than to pull this shit with him. He glanced at the clock, a bit surprised to see it so late, but with a sigh, he stood and walked upstairs to Ash's room. He knocked lightly on the door while opening it, knowing Ash should be asleep by now, and smiled seeing the boy passed out on the bed, his cell in hand having fallen asleep waiting for Liam to answer him. He moved over to the bed quietly, put the phone on the nightstand and covered him with the blanket. He glanced around the room, a small shiver having gone through him, before he headed out of the room, turning off the light and shutting the door behind him.

Stavros glanced around the hallway, feeling rage building up in him but he pushed that aside. With a heavy sigh, he locked up the house quickly and went to his own room.

☽ CHAPTER TWENTY ☾

"Dad," Ash whispered, shaking his dad softly. "Dad!" he yelled after a few moments, shaking him more violently.

Stavros snapped open his eyes, groaning as he sat up, "Ash?" he asked, confused, as he glanced at the time. "It's 3am. What are you doing awake?" he asked, keeping the blanket wrapped around himself as he stood.

Before Ash could answer a loud knock sounded on the front door again. Frowning, Stavros was quick to pull on some pants, making a small mental note to maybe not sleep naked anymore, and looked at Ash, "Wait here," he said firmly.

He walked down the stairs, turning on the lights as he went, and unlocked the front door, turning on the porch light as he opened it. He blinked as he looked at two cops standing there.

"Mr. Morana?" one asked.

"Yes?"

"I'm officer Kyle Skilts. I have the understanding that you were close with Mr. Tase and his son Liam?" the officer asked.

"Liam?" Ash said, standing at the top of the stairs, because of course, he didn't listen. "Yes. Why? What happened?"

"Ash, please." Stavros said, looking over his shoulder at him, he was worried about Ash hearing this. He turned his attention back to the officers. "Yes. Has something happened?"

Officer Kyle let out a slow breath while nodding, "May we come in?" he asked. "Yes, of course." Stavros said, stepping back to allow them inside.

The Officers stepped inside and shut the door behind them as Kyle gestured for Stavros to take a seat on the couch.

Ash watched from the stairs as they walked into the livingroom and then quickly ran down the stairs to stand in the doorway.

Stavros glanced at Ash, "Go to your room, Ash." His voice held no room for argument.

Ash clenched his jaw, wanting to argue since this was about his friend, but he knew it was wise not to. He headed upstairs, cursing under his breath but he sat down on the top step instead of going to his room.

"We got a call a few hours ago. A neighbor heard yelling coming from Mr. Tase's house and when we arrived we found Mr. Tase's dead body in Liam's room" officer Kyle explained, opening his mouth to speak more but Ash was suddenly there.

"What about Liam?" Ash asked, having practically jumped from the top step hearing about Dan's dead body.

"Ash!" Stavros snapped, narrowing his eyes on him. He wanted to strangle the boy but at the same time, he understood. This was about Ash's best friend, after all, and he was positive Ash would be hearing this soon enough anyways.

"We haven't found Liam." Kyle said, turning to look at Ash. "We found Dan in Liam's room, but no Liam anywhere." he said softly. Kyle turned his brown eyes towards Stavros, "I'm not sure it's wise for him to be down here listening to this."

Stavros sighed heavily, "He can stay. He'll find this all out anyways and knowing Liam is missing, he'll never leave."

Ash choked back a sob and stared at the officer for a few minutes trying to figure out what he had said. He heard his father speaking but didn't hear a thing that was said. Liam was missing? What happened?

Where did he go? Was Liam dead too? Ash felt his heart quicken, felt the familiar tightness in his chest, he couldn't breathe. Everything around him was starting to fade and it wasn't until his father was right in front of him, hugging him tight and rubbing his back, that he realized he had been gasping for breath and tears were rolling down his cheeks. "Breathe." Stavros said, his voice calm and soothing. "I got you," he whispered. He felt his son trembling in his arms so he just kept rubbing his back and holding him. Stavros glanced over at the officer, "I hadn't realized Dan was home." he said softly. "Last I heard of him, he was in rehab."

"When was that?" Kyle asked softly, concern on his face as he looked at Ash. "We can come back.." he added.

"Two weeks ago Sunday." Stavros responded.

Ash was starting to calm down, feeling safe and having time to collect himself in his fathers arms.

"When did you last see Liam?" Kyle asked, writing down some notes.

"Sunday. He came by looking for Ash but he wasn't here so I drove him home. He didn't say anything about his father being back but I could tell something was wrong." Stavros said. "Do you know of any places Liam would run off to?" Kyle asked.

Stavros cleared his throat and shook his head "You think Liam did it." it wasn't a question. Officer Kyle tensed for a moment, giving a small shake of his head "We aren't jumping to anything. We asked around about the family and checked out his moms house but he wasn't there. She informed us that Mr. Tase is an abusive drunk. In cases like these the victim can snap and lose control of their actions to defend themselves."

Ash shook his head quickly, pulling away from his dad to glare at the cop, "Not Liam. His father was getting help. My dad paid for his rehab! He was getting help and Liam was all excited about it and was even making plans for them to just move on from the past and they were going to be happy and father and son again and.. And.. and Liam wouldn't do this!" Ash choked out, his breathing hitching at such a thought. He wouldn't believe it, he couldn't, Liam was his best friend and the most gentle person he has ever known! It wasn't in Liam to kill his father. Hell the boy wasn't even able to kill a spider!

"Ash." Stavros said calmly. "Calm down, breathe." he soothed, keeping a hand on his shoulder. "Do you know where Liam is?" he asked.

Ash shook his head quickly, his thoughts racing all over the place, "I-I-I don't um.. I don't know.. He hasn't been answering my texts or calls. He hasn't been in school for a few days.. He.." he felt like the world was spinning. What if Liam was dead too? What if these asshole cops found him and locked him up forever without searching for the truth? "What if Liam is missing? What if whoever got his father took him too?" Ash whispered. "What about Patrick? He was supposed to be taking care of Liam, what if Patrick did this? Or Tyler?" Ash asked, looking up at his father. "I knew those two were bad news, I knew something was off about them but everyone told me not to worry! That I was just imagining things!" He pushed away from his father, angrily wiping the tears from his cheeks.

"Who is Tyler and Patrick?" Kyle asked, frowning.

"Tyler was the man who took Dan to rehab, Patrick was watching over Liam." Stavros explained, turning to face him.

Officer Kyle raised a brow at the new information and began writing more notes down. "I'll look into Patrick and Tyler, do you know their last names or where I can find them?" he asked.

Stavros gave a shake of his head, "I have no idea where they would have gone and I honestly can't recall their last names." he said. He saw Ash looking at him from the corner of his eye, knowing his son caught onto his lie easily since Stavros didn't forget things.

Stavros looked at Ash, "Do you have any ideas of where Liam would have gone?" he asked. He knew the answer to that already, it'd be yes, but he wasn't going to be surprised if Ash lied.

Of course Ash knew many places Liam could go to but he was not about to tell them any of that. "He could have gone anywhere. He could have gone to his mothers or maybe he could have gone under the bridge where a lot of kids like to hang out." Ash spoke quickly, knowing by the looks on their faces none of them believed him. He couldn't get his thoughts straight though and he couldn't tell them without knowing what they'd do to Liam if they found him. He just couldn't wrap his head around all of this. How could he? He was worried about Liam enough as it was and now.. Now his father was dead and he was officially missing? How could that be possible?. Stavros watched the pain going through Ash and reached over to take his hand "it's okay, Ash. We'll find Liam. He couldn't have gone far." he said soothingly.

Ash nodded quickly "We'll find him" he whispered. They had to find him and protect him because there was no doubt in his mind that somehow Patrick and Tyler caused this.

"If you do happen to find him please call me or bring him to the police station." Kyle said as he held out his card to Stavros. "I'm very sorry for your loss," he said.

"Losing Dan is nothing," Ash said, a bitter tone in his voice. He had no love for that man and was thankful he was dead. "We just have to find Liam. He wouldn't have done this. I don't care what you assholes think! Liam wouldn't have done this." Ash snapped, running up to his room and slamming his door.

Stavros stepped forward, "Ash." He said sternly, sighing when he went running up to his room. He took the card from Kyle and set it on the table. "I'm sorry about that, officer Kyle" he said as he walked him to the door.

Kyle shook his head "Don't be. I know this must be hard for him. We need to understand what happened at Mr. Tase's house and we need to find Liam. We don't know if he is injured or if he is the one who caused his father's death. We need to find him" he said, determined to find out the truth.

Stavros nodded "If we find him we will call you" he assured. He opened the door and rubbed his face as the officers walked out to their car and drove off. Stavros closed and locked the front door, sighing heavily before he headed right up to Ash room. He knocked on the door and loudly called out, "Are you okay?" stupid question, he knew the answer. Stavros was about to call out again but Ash opened his door.

"No," Ash whispered, staring at the ground. "They think Liam killed his dad. He wouldn't have done it. I know he wouldn't have done it. He couldn't have." Ash said, slowly walking back to his bed and sitting on it. "He was so excited, So excited for his dad to get clean. I know he tried not to get too hopeful but he did." Ash said, looking at his dad as Stavros walked into the room and sat beside him. Ash stood up and started pacing, "How could this happen? What if Liam got hurt? What if he's dead?" Ash's voice cracked as he spoke, more tears rolling down his cheeks. He gripped at his hair, just wanting to scream his frustration.

Stavros stood and gently touched his shoulder, "Deep breaths, Ash. Don't think about that okay? Just keep telling yourself that he is fine and alive. We'll find him." he said softly.

Ash's breathing was shaky as he glared at his father, his hands dropping from his hair to his sides, "You lied to those cops. You said you didn't know their last name but I know you do." he said, his anger rising.

"You also lied to them, Ash, you know all the places Liam would have run off too." Stavros responded, keeping his voice level despite his own anger creeping up.

"Why'd you leave him alone with Patrick?" Ash demanded, "I said something felt wrong about those two, but you, Lucian, and Dakota said it was nothing, that they were trustworthy." his body started to tremble as he spoke, "Did you know they would do this? Did they kill Liam too and we just haven't found his body? Are they responsible for all those other deaths too?" Ash snapped, his voice rising with each question. "Is Liam dead?!" he shouted when he didn't get an answer. Stavros let out a slow breath, understanding Ash was angry and lashing out, "We don't know if Liam is dead and I have no answers for your questions, Ash, calm down." he warned.

"Calm down? My best friend might be dead right now because you're too fucking stupid to listen to me when I-" Ash's shouting was cut short when a sudden pain exploded in his cheek. Ash actually stumbled from the backhand, more tears forming in his eyes as he reached a hand up to rub his throbbing cheek.

Stavros had tried keeping his own temper in check, he really tried. He knew Ash was afraid and hurting so he understood his lashing out, but being called 'fucking stupid' crossed a line that made his own anger erupt. Stavros hand throbbed a bit in pain, and for a moment he just stood there in silence staring at the boy. "It's getting late," he finally said, his tone a lot sharper than he had wanted it to be. "We will look for Liam in the morning. Get some sleep." Without waiting for a response, he left the room. Stavros ran his fingers through his hair as he walked down the steps, so badly needing a coffee right now.

Ash didn't say a word, didn't even move until his father left the room. A sob left him as he walked over to his bed, still rubbing his cheek but he knew he shouldn't have freaked out like that on his dad. Stavros wouldn't have done anything to put Liam in danger, right? Ash shut his eyes to force himself to calm down, wanting to stop crying and to think clearly. He swallowed, opening his eyes with a frown at the taste of blood in his mouth. Carefully, Ash moved his tongue around and realized his tooth must have cut his cheek when he got hit.

Ash didn't bother changing his clothes or even turning off his light, he just laid down and quietly cried himself to sleep.

Stavros sat at the table, staring down at his coffee and getting lost in his own thoughts when his cell rang. Without even needing to check who was calling, he answered "What have you done?" he snapped, his anger rising all over again. He walked to his office and shut the door behind him, "What do you mean? 'Nothing?' I know what happened so far since the police were just at my fucking house." he hissed through his teeth. He growled loudly as he listened to the voice and rubbed his temples "I'm telling you both to stop. Now. You are to pick up and leave." he ordered. He gripped his phone so hard in his hand it almost broke, "Why? You are seriously asking me why? Because, you fucking shitstain, you've caused more trouble than you should have." he hissed. "Bring Liam to me, Stay away from my son. Pack your shit and get out of here. I will not tell you again." he spat and snapped his cell shut. He let out a slow breath to calm himself and then walked over to his desk, sat down, and rubbed his face. He cursed at himself remembering he left his coffee in the kitchen so he got up and just as he opened the door, he saw Ash walking past.

"Where are you going?" Stavros asked, stepping out of his office.

"I can't sit here and wait. I have to find him. I can't leave him alone." Ash said. He got his shoes on and looked at his father "I'm going whether you want me to or not so you can either come with me or just sit here but I'm going." He yanked his jacket from the closet and reached for the door.

Stavros cursed under his breath and grabbed Ash's arm "*We* will go together." He said. He was about to put on his shoes but then remembered he was only wearing pants, "Let me change quickly and then we will go." he said. He knew this was probably a bad idea but he couldn't let Ash go alone and he honestly didn't feel like having to watch him all night just to make sure he didn't sneak out.

Stavros wasted no time changing and once he made sure he had all he needed, he headed out the door with Ash. He locked up the house and glanced at Ash, who looked like he was so lost in deep thought, "Where should we look first?" he asked, slipping into his car and starting it.

Ash shrugged, "He could have gone to the cliff. We like hanging out there at times. We can look under the bridge next." he said. He got into the front and buckled up, staring out the window and hoping they would find him.

Stavros nodded and started to drive, "We will look for a few hours but do not panic if we don't find him."

Ash gave a nod but he had no idea if he'd even be able to do that. He had so many things running through his mind right now and he couldn't sort any of it out no matter how hard he tried.

☽ CHAPTER TWENTY-ONE ☾

Tyler threw his cell at the wall, growling in anger and pacing back and forth. He was still at Dan's, having stayed hidden when the cops arrived. He knew pushing things the way they had would have pissed the man off. Great. With a heavy sigh, he faded from the room and appeared in a white mist outside the hotel room Patrick was in. Tyler knocked on the door, stepping inside once Patrick opened the door and sighed heavily, "You aren't going to like this." he warned. "We need to leave." he said, glancing over at Liam who looked to be sleeping on a twin bed.

"What? Why? I'm not done with my food" Patrick said, crossing his arms.

"We have been ordered to leave, Pat. You know we can't stay now." Tyler said. "We can just leave him here and go somewhere else." He knew Patrick wouldn't like it but there wasn't anything they could do about that.

Patrick growled at that, "No. I'm not leaving. I put too much time and effort into this boy, he's mine." he snapped.

"Damnit, Patrick! This isn't a battle we can win and pissing the man off even more will make things worse. We'll leave and find you a new toy to play with."

Patrick narrowed his eyes, wanting to just go over to Liam now and rip him to shreds but he knew Tyler was correct, they couldn't get into a fight and expect to win against him. With a snarl, Pat turned and stomped out of the room, needing a minute to calm down before he did something really stupid.

Hissing under his breath, "Fucking asshole ruining my fun."

As he walked, kicking at the snow, he bitched under his breath about how unfair things were as he turned into an alley. By now it was almost 5am and the town was still quiet, no doubt because of the lockdown.

"Oh Patty," echoed a deep and sing-song voice.

Stopping dead in his tracks, Patrick looked around quickly to see who had just spoken, but he saw no one.

"Someone's been naughty," the voice taunted.

While he was looking around, Patrick didn't notice that it started getting darker in the alley. "Who's there?" Patrick growled. It wasn't often someone could sneak up on him, he was a demon, after all. Patrick heard chuckling around him and took a few steps back, tensing when he backed into something solid. He thought it was the wall at first, until he felt a warm breath on the back of his neck. Patrick spun around quickly, his eyes widening as he looked up at the tall man who had glowing red eyes. It was like Patrick forgot how to breathe while staring up at this giant of a man, any light around them seemed to have vanished.

"S-Sh-Shadow" Patrick breathed out, panic and fear filling his voice.

Shadow's hand shot out and gripped Patrick's throat tightly, his long claws digging into the man's neck as he slammed him against the wall, pinning him there, his feet dangling off the ground as he was slowly lifted.

Shadow smirked, leaning closer to Patrick's face, so close they were almost touching, so close that Patrick could feel the warmth of his breath.

"It's Lord, to you, Patty." Shadow's voice was almost a whisper but filled with amusement. His other hand reached up, lightly running his claws along Patrick's jaw.

Patrick gripped Shadow's wrist tightly, wanting to pull free from him but also too terrified to move.

Shadow patted Patrick's cheek before releasing him, letting the man fall to his feet while taking a step back.

"I hear you may be packing up and leaving," he said, examining his claws like he was bored. Patrick instantly dropped to his knees when he was released and kept his head bowed, resisting the urge to rub his throbbing neck, "Yes, Lord, we've-"

"You look so delightful down on your knees." Shadow cut in, his voice taunting before sighing. "I know why you are leaving." He said, chuckling. "You're going to finish the job you started." his tone became deadly serious.

Patrick shuddered at his first comment, sure, he enjoyed the company of men and women but he didn't imagine he'd be living after having Shadow's company. With wide eyes, Patrick looked up at him, "I can't, we are under orders-"

"I just gave you new orders," Shadow snarled sharply, his eyes narrowing ever so slightly as a dark mist formed around Pat's neck, taking the solid form of a collar. Reaching to grasp it til Shadow jerked the leash attached, forcing the man onto his tiptoes, "You will do what I ordered." Patrick grunted softly, trying not to fall into Shadow. "I'll be killed," he whispered.

Shadow tsked softly, "You can either devour Liam like planned and have a fitting last meal, or run but if you do decide to run, just know, you'll still be hunted down like the filthy dog you are." he purred, flashing his fangs in a smirk.

"Why is it so important to you? Why are you even here-" he was cut off as all the air left his lungs, his back slammed against the wall, Shadow's fingers wrapped tightly around his neck, scared one wrong move would snap it.

"Do not question me, pet" Shadow snapped.

"You do as told-" his face inches away from the smaller demon "-or pay the price for defining me, I have no such compunction to care for a dog like you" Shadows fangs peeked from under his lips.

Pat held tightly to his wrist trying to pull the man's hand from his neck. "It's Patrick, I'm no one's fucking pet!" Pat couldn't stop himself as he lifted his leg and went to collide his knee into the Lord's side, hissing in pain feeling like he hit a rock. Distracted by the pain and fear running through him, he didn't realize that his throat was now released and his hands pinned above his head. It all happened so fast and it took a moment for Pat to process that it was a black tendril pinning him, not Shadow's hand.

Shadow's smile grew into a sinister grin as he watched the man with wide black eyes, his red pupils dilated. "Oh?" his free hand had stopped the stupid pet's actions as he gripped the knee, his grip tightening in warning. Black shadows enveloped Pat's leg keeping it up and open for him to slip between and closer to him. He leaned in closer, his lips brushing against Patrick's ear "soon, you'll understand why that, my pet, isn't true"

Patrick went cold feeling the bulge pushing up against his own, there was no way in his mind that this was fucking happening "Get the fuck away from m-" he was cut off as his head snapped to the side, the sting of Shadows back hand giving him a grim reminder of his position here. "You will ask to speak to me"

Pat could taste the copper on his tongue as his hazel eyes turned yellow, the color bleeding into the white of his eyes, glaring up at the man that held his leash. "Good~" he purred as his claws ran up the man's leg, ripping the denim like it was paper, nicking his skin leaving a small red line as blood bubbled to the surface.

"Don't worry, this won't hurt nearly as much as it will if you defy me," Shadow's head tilted as he watched his own work, admiring the small cut his claws made over the man's skin. The fabric falling away from Pat's leg and his waist, barely clinging on to his other leg.

Pats heart raced within his chest, he never felt panic like this before, never felt so damn fucking small but he would be damned to make this easy. He went to move but stopped mid movement as a sharp black needle like tendril stopped centimeters away from his eye, "Don't think about it Pet" Shadows voice purred as his body seemed to melt away, his hold replaced by the shadows "I don't want to ruin my fun to fast~" the black tendril slowly thickens as it slithers over his mouth. A chuckle echoed around him as Pat's eyes darted around, looking for the Lord as he panted heavily against the shadow over his lips. "Yes, little pet, try and figure out an escape" Shadow's voice mocked.

He tugged against the tendril, shifting his body to fight against the shadows as muffled grunts escaped him.

"It's strange, you seemed stronger than this. " He provoked the demon as he appeared behind him. Feeling the hands sliding around his waist, Pat realized he was no longer pinned to the wall, but suspended mid-air by the tendril and completely at Shadow's mercy. The fear almost crippled Pat as he fully realized he was now exposed to his gaze, a shiver ran up his spine feeling Shadow's tongue lick at his neck.

"You won't enjoy this" Shadow lowly moaned against Pat's ear. "But I will, pet."

Screams muffled against the tendril over Pat's mouth, his chest tightening as fear overwhelmed him. Pat felt the tip of Shadows cock press at his entrance, with no warning his body was forcefully entered, his eyes wide as white hot pain shot through his body making his back arch away from his assailant. Shadow moaned in satisfaction hearing the muffled pain-filled screams, his grip tight on his waist, pulling him back into him.

"Blood always makes the best lube," Shadow moaned into Pat's ear before he sank his fangs into the demon's neck and picked up a ruthless rhythm.

The shadow over his mouth pushed between his lips, pushing deep into his throat making him choke for air. His body forced him to gag, trying to expel the thing in his throat but it was of no use, even biting down was seemingly useless to stop the assault.

Shadow growled with enjoyment, feeling his pet's body trembling, intensified his pleasure, causing his pace to quicken.

Removing his fangs, he chuckled darkly into his ear, "Bite all you wish, pet, it won't save you" His claws piercing deep into Pat's skin, blood pooling at the surface.

Patrick closed his eyes tightly, whimpering as a few small tears rolled down his cheeks, knowing there was no escape, he walked into the spider's web and would pay for it.

☽ CHAPTER TWENTY-TWO ☾

It was near 9 in the morning when Ash and his father returned home. They had no luck finding Liam and he still wasn't answering his cell. Ash tried not thinking of the worst things possible but it was hard and the longer he didn't hear from Liam, the harder it was to keep positive. Ash went straight up to his room and plugged his cell in to charge before sitting on his bed and rubbing his face. He was exhausted and knew he had to get some sleep but part of him was afraid he'd wake up to knocking on his door and finding out that Liam was found dead somewhere. He had no idea where Liam would have gone since he wasn't in the normal hide-outs.

"Are you doing okay?" Stavros asked from the doorway.

Ash shook his head but didn't speak, he just stared down at his hands and was trying not to cry. Stavros frowned as he walked into the room and sat down beside him, "We'll find him. Okay?

You need to try getting some sleep now and when you wake up we'll get something to eat and go looking for him again." he promised.

Ash gave a weak smile, "Okay" he whispered. He stared at his cell for a few moments but when nothing happened he just laid down on the bed and sighed heavily while shutting his eyes. He felt the bed shift as his father stood, opening his eyes, he sat up on his elbows and looked at him, "I know you are hiding something from me." he said.

Stavros almost groaned in annoyance at Ash's words, "What makes you think that?" he asked. "Because you refuse to tell me anything about Patrick and Tyler. You refuse to even talk about them now." Ash replied, shifting on his bed so he was sitting up fully.

Stavros let out a slow breath, turning to fully face Ash, "What do you want me to say, Ash?." he asked, crossing his arms. "It's clear that no matter what I say you won't believe it anyways." Ash shrugged at that, "I'd say the truth, but you clearly don't know what that is."

"Watch yourself." Stavros warned, his voice stern.

Stavros watched Ash for a minute, he knew this was hard on the boy, that he wanted answers, that he was overwhelmed with worry for his best friend but Stavros couldn't tell him the truth, not yet.

Ash said nothing because he knew the next words out of his mouth would not be kind and, even though he was angry that his dad was hiding something from him, it wouldn't be right to take his anger out on his father.

Stavros went to his own room without saying another word to Ash and called his school to explain why he wouldn't be there, not that it fully mattered since most parents were keeping their children home now. Knowing he wouldn't be able to sleep, he went downstairs to make himself some coffee.

Ash woke up around 2pm to the sound of his cell going off. He groaned, his body and mind not ready to be awake but wanting to check the time anyway, he rolled over to grab it, sitting up quickly when he saw the time. "Fuck," he groaned, now wishing he remembered to set an alarm, but that thought quickly left his mind seeing a message from Liam.

'I'm okay. Don't look for me.'

It's all the message said and Ash read it about a thousand times. He tried calling Liam and sending a lot of text but he didn't get any responses. He growled in frustration and walked to his window. He stared out, half hoping that Liam would be standing outside waving at him to come out but there was nothing, not even the normal traffic. Ash sighed and decided it was best to just take a shower and eat some food so he could take time to clear his head and talk with his dad about the next plan. He knew if Liam didn't want to be found he wouldn't be in his normal hiding spots. Ash heard some banging in the kitchen, knowing it was his father making food, but he ignored his hunger for now, even though his mouth watered at the smell of bacon. He gathered up a change of clothes, leaving his room to take his shower. The school dance was that Friday but he knew there was no way he was going to it if they hadn't found Liam.

Stavros decided to make some bacon and eggs with toast, when he was about to go wake up Ash but he heard the shower running. He knew Ash needed to get a bit more sleep so he hoped eating would make him tired enough, but knowing Ash was worried about Liam, he wouldn't be sleeping anymore until he was found. Stavros had tried calling Patrick and Tyler but none answered, which was starting to piss him off, but caring for Ash and his well-being was the only thing he cared about. Stavros just finished putting the food on the table when the shower turned off and a few minutes later he heard Ash leave the bathroom. He sat down and sipped his coffee and was joined by Ash a few moments later.

Ash sat at the table and poked at his eggs with his fork. He was starving and knew he had to eat but the thought of eating also made him feel sick. "Liam sent me a text," he said softly, breaking the silence.

Stavros raised a brow, "Oh? What did he say?" "That he is okay and not to look for him."

"Do you believe him?"

Ash sighed, leaning back in his chair, while putting his fork down, "I honestly don't know. I don't know what to think about any of this. I didn't even know his dad was home from rehab. Liam doesn't normally keep things from me and I don't understand why he didn't tell me." He rambled, his emotions getting high. Ash took a second to calm himself, inhaling deeply, "I just want to know what's going on with him and what happened." He said, exhaling slowly.

Stavros nodded, watching his son, "Well if he doesn't want to be found we won't find him." "I can't stop looking for him." Ash said, determined.

"I did not say we'd stop looking for him." Stavros clarified, "I'm saying take the rest of today to gather your thoughts and think about places he'd go so he can't be found."

Ash didn't like the idea of just sitting here and doing nothing but his dad was right, he had to think of places Liam would go that were hidden, even from him.

Ash pushed away from the table, about to head upstairs but stopped when his dad spoke. "You need to eat, Ash. You haven't eaten all day."

Ash let out a long breath, wishing he could just hide away right now but his father was right, he needed to eat. Pulling himself closer to the table, he remained silent as he began to eat.

They remained silent while they ate, Ash forced himself to eat at least half before he went upstairs to his room. Ash didn't bother laying down, even with his body begging him to, he sat at his desk and pulled up maps of the area on his laptop.

Stavros cleaned up the kitchen when Ash left and went to his office, sighing seeing he still had no response from the brothers. Stavros needed all this bullshit to end, needed it to be over, so Ash wouldn't be suffering anymore. He wanted to help his son through all of this but he knew, at least right now, he was making it worse. Stavros ran a hand through his hair, leaning back in his chair with his eyes closed, frustrated that the two brothers weren't listening to a fucking word he said anymore. He wasn't used to people not listening to him so this was a new feeling, an odd feeling, to him.

"Dad?" Ash called out, walking down the stairs, "I think I know where Liam might be.. Normally we'd go hide out by the cliffs but if he doesn't want to be found he could be hiding out further down them around the waterfall."

Stavros stepped out of his office hearing his son's words, giving a nod as he listened, "We can look." he said. "If he isn't there, we'll come back home and try again tomorrow. Now go get ready."

Ash rushed upstairs for his cell, came back down, and pulled on his coat and boots, there wasn't much snow on the ground yet but it was colder out now. Once they both were ready, Stavros followed Ash outside and to the car.

Stavros knew this was going to be a waste of time but he wouldn't stop Ash from looking and he wasn't about to let him go off alone.

It was just under thirty minutes when Stavros pulled into the parking lot of a few shady shops. One store was a pawn shop, which was the closest to the cliff, but it had boards up on the window since someone had thrown bricks at it a few weeks back. A clothing store was beside it but it was going out of business so there was a '50% off' sign in the window to get rid of the clothing still inside. A book store was beside that but it had been broken into a week ago by some punks who decided to set a bunch of books on fire so it was still getting fixed up. This wasn't an area that Stavros liked his son being in because it was on the outskirts of town, too close to the cliffs, and just a very unpleasant area.

Stavros got out of the car and looked around, listening closely to see if anyone was around. The area was surrounded by a lot of trees and was so far from the center of town, he wondered why they even bothered building this stripmall. He knew there was a time they planned on expanding their small town but it lost funding. Most teens loved to hang out in the woods and cause all kinds of trouble; however park rangers tried putting a stop to that by going through the woods and threatening to fine anyone they saw, it did help to keep people out of the deeper parts of the woods. Pushing those thoughts from his mind, he walked beside Ash up the path to the cliff, stopping at the tree line.

Ash shivered just a little from a cold breeze as he walked on the trail towards the falls. He looked around the whole time, hoping he'd catch sight of Liam. He heard the low rumble from the falls just ahead of them and remembered the first time he and Liam stumbled upon it. It was an early summer morning and they were about ten years old. They had seen deer walking through the woods that day and heard all the birds singing, smelt the flowers and grass. It was really beautiful and they even went swimming at the falls. The water came down from a mountain, they never went to the top but near the bottom was a lake that was great for swimming and even fishing at the right time of year. They went back there many times after that day.

Stavros stopped once they arrived and looked around but he saw nothing and all he could hear was the water flowing. Stavros glanced down at Ash and saw the hope get crushed in his eyes but there wasn't anything he could do about that. "He isn't here."

Ash shook his head, "He could be somewhere.."

"Ash." Stavros said, his voice calm. "There is no place around here that would keep him warm. He'd end up freezing. He wouldn't come out here before a snow storm." he explained.

Ash wanted to scream in frustration but he knew it'd solve nothing. He could spend hours looking everywhere around here but he knew his father was right, Liam hated the cold and wouldn't be out here even if it was to hide. He gave a nod and followed his dad back to the car.

☽ CHAPTER TWENTY-THREE ☾

Patrick's body throbbed in pain as he laid on the ground, bloodied and bruised. He had no idea when Shadow had actually left but he wasn't going to wait around here long enough for the asshole to come back. He hissed in pain as he slowly got up, using the wall for support as he struggled up onto his feet. His legs buckled, causing him to fall to his knees with a curse. Letting out a sharp breath, he got himself back to his feet. A shudder of disgust went through him feeling something dripping down his leg, he could guess what it was but he wasn't going to look to confirm it. Patrick didn't bother trying to cover himself up since he wasn't far from the room anyways. He had to hold onto the wall, knowing he'd fall if he didn't, he clenched his jaw tightly from the pain that soared through his body from walking. Patrick finally got to the hotel room and nearly fell flat on his face as he stumbled through the door. He glanced around quickly, relaxing just slightly seeing Liam was still fast asleep on the bed, but he didn't see Tyler. He was actually thankful for that since he honestly didn't want to get into what fucking happened. Pat stumbled to the bathroom and locked the door behind him. He started up the shower, making sure the water was scolding hot, and removed what was left of his clothes. Patrick made sure to not even look down at himself, not needing to see the bruises or other marks on him, he felt them and was very well aware they were there. He stepped into the shower, hissing from the sting of the water hitting his wounds, and didn't leave the shower until the water started running cold. He made sure to scrub every inch of him over and over again, not caring of the pain it caused himself, it just fueled his inner rage.

Tyler was back by the time Patrick left the bathroom and scowled seeing the state he was in. "I know you were pissed, but did you really storm off to fuck someone?" Tyler asked, rolling his eyes.

"What?" Patrick asked, having not heard a word he said.

Tyler watched Pat move around the room, grabbing clothes to get dressed in.

"You have bruises and scratch marks all over you, how'd you even find someone to bang anyways? It's dead out there." Tyler said.

Patrick's lip went up in a snarl at Tyler's words but he kept his back to him, "I find my ways." was all he said before he went back to the bathroom to dress.

"So," Tyler started once Pat walked out, "Where have you been?"

Patrick went to the bed and laid down on it, not sure sitting was the best idea currently. "I was around." he murmured.

Tyler just sighed, having no idea what was wrong with his brother but it was clear he was in a bitter mood.

"Are we just leaving Liam here?" Tyler asked.

Patrick actually glared at Tyler, "No. We are finishing this like planned."

"We can't-"

"I'm not arguing about this." Patrick cut in, his voice a low growl. "Trust me, okay? This will be done as planned."

"Trust you?" Tyler scoffed, "how will we keep doing this and avoid the asshole?"

"We just will. He's busy with other shit anyways." Patrick said simply. "Now shut up so I can sleep." he murmured, closing his eyes and turning on his side away from Tyler.

Tyler returned a few hours later, having left once Patrick went to sleep, it was his turn to calm down from Patrick's stupidity and he also wanted to check around to make sure they were still hidden. When he returned, Liam was sitting on a chair, hugging his knees to his chest and just staring at the ground and Patrick was pacing around and cursing.

"How's it going in here?" Tyler asked, taking off his shoes.

"It's going fine. Or at least it would be if Liam would stop crying and panicking about all this." Patrick grumbled.

"I told you not to push him too much too fast." Tyler replied. "You could have very well ruined your supper."

Patrick stopped pacing, "He isn't ruined. He just needs to be reminded of why he asked for my help."

Tyler chuckled, "I don't think that is the problem. I think all he is remembering is how you helped him. "

"Shut up." Patrick hissed. "You're the one who killed his father right in front of him." "You told me to."

"I didn't tell you to do it right in front of the boy."

Tyler stood slowly and stretched, "True but you could have easily taken him somewhere else. Now stop playing with your dinner. Cops are everywhere and soon we are going to be hunted as well."

"Human's have no chance of finding us."

"I'm not talking about humans." Tyler growled. "We went against orders. You know we were supposed to leave but you refused so now we need to just hurry up so we don't end up dead." Patrick crossed his arms over his chest, "You are a huge coward for a demon.."

Tyler narrowed his eyes, "I'm not a coward. You know who he is and what he is and we have no chance of beating that."

Patrick shook his head, "Yeah, Yeah. Whatever." Patrick looked over at Liam as he walked to him and lightly tapped on his head, "Liam? You can't stay hiding in there all day."

Patrick held back a groan of annoyance when Liam didn't even move. He crouched down in front of him, "Are you planning on snapping out of this any time soon?"

Again no answer.

Patrick wanted to strangle him. He forced the boy to look up at him, "Anyone alive in there?"

Liam swatted Patrick's hand away, "Go away."

"Oh my Lord, he spoke!." Patrick gasped. "Here I thought the cat did catch your tongue." Liam rolled his eyes, "What?"

"You know that stupid saying? 'Cat got your tongue?'" Liam just sighed and shut his eyes.

"You can't be sitting here all day doing nothing. We have things to do, remember? Those bullies aren't gonna lay down and die just for you."

Liam didn't say anything at first, his mind going back and remembering those billies from public school. He remembered how they tormented him, shoving him to the ground, beating his ass, or even locking him in a locker for a few hours. They have given Liam a black eye and even broke his nose before Ash showed up, new to the school, and chased them off. Every once in a while they bullies do call Liam names and try getting under his skin but but with Ash around, they dare not touch him again and fuck with him too badly.

"Go away." Liam muttered, remembering Pat had spoken to him.

Patrick frowned as he stood up and tilted his head. He looked the pathetic human over slowly and sighed heavily in annoyance.

Liam's hair was all messy and his body still had some bruises. Patrick could heal the wounds but he didn't want to. Liam now had a tattoo on the left side of his neck, it was a storm cloud with lightning bolts coming down with the sun peaking through, it matched one on Patrick's neck. It was a way for a demon to show who the human belonged to. Not all demons marked their food but Patrick wasn't risking some other snot nose demon coming along and stealing his hard earned meal.

Patrick reached down and grabbed Liam's upper arm, quickly jerking him up to his feet. He released him, chuckling while Liam cursed, stumbling forward, losing his footing, and fell to the floor.

"Oh good. You're up. Now get plotting your revenge against those horrible bullies like a good little bad boy so I can kill them and leave."

Liam flipped him off as he stood, muttering to himself as he went to the bathroom. He was struggling with grasping everything that was going on at the moment. He was with two demons and one had killed his father a day ago, or was it two days? Maybe a week ago? He had no idea anymore. He had tried asking questions about the demons but they didn't seem happy about answering, in fact, they had been really annoyed and threatened to remove his tongue many times. He was told the cops were looking for him and he had wanted to call Ash just to explain what happened but Patrick had taken his phone and told him not to worry about that stuff right now.

Liam had gathered some information when he heard Patrick and Tyler talking last night but all he found out was that they needed to leave town quickly before the demon Lord in this town found them. He guessed they were doing things against the rules or something. When Liam first came here he spent the first few hours getting sick and when he found out the cops were looking for him, wanting to question him about his father's death, he broke down and cried for a while, begging Patrick to fix everything that had happened. It was Tyler who snapped at him about being weak and that his father had been a good meal, that he should stop crying like a baby. After that Liam spent most of his time lying in that bed and ignoring the outside world.

Liam walked out of the bathroom and flopped down onto the chair, glaring at the two demons. "Finally he honors us with his presence." Tyler mused.

Patrick leaned against the wall and half shrugged, "He wanted to be a baby about it but I snapped him out of that."

"I am right here." Liam hissed.

"Do you think he'll start crying again?" Tyler asked. "Because that was really annoying." "I hope not. I might have to remove his eyes to stop it if he does." Patrick replied.

Tyler chuckled, "That could actually be fun. You should try that.. Maybe we can spoon them out.."

Patrick shook his head, "Why use a spoon? I got claws, that'd be a lot more fun to use." "That is true."

"I'M.RIGHT.HERE." Liam snapped. "And you can't spoon my eyes out."

Tyler glanced over at Liam and slowly raised a brow, "I could too. You aren't much of a fighter, it'd be so easy."

"Leave him alone, Tyler. He's grumpy." Patrick teased. "How do humans stop being grumpy?" "We could try hitting him really hard..."

"Dan did that a lot and it didn't seem to help." "What about sleep?"

"No, he's had enough sleep.. Food?" Patrick suggested, looking at Liam. "Are you hungry, little pet?"

Liam clenched his jaw and counted to ten to keep from snapping at the morons. "I'm not a pet." he hissed through his clenched teeth.

Patrick's eyes darkened at those words but forced those memories out of his mind and shrugged, "You are pretty much. I have to feed you, take you on walks, make sure you get sleep and have a bath.."

"I can do that all by myself." "Fine."

Liam stood up and walked to the small kitchen setup the hotel room had, fighting the urge to punch Patrick. He opened the mini fridge and blinked seeing it was empty. He started opening cupboards and saw they were all empty too. "You didn't get any food?"

"I thought you could do this all yourself?"

Liam slammed the cupboard shut and tried weighing his options. He could always punch Patrick but the guy was a demon so that would likely end up with him losing his hands. They did not like it when people spoke loudly around them so screaming at them was a bad choice too.

Liam let out a real slow breath, "Can you just answer the question?" "We don't have food because we don't eat food."

"How did you plan on feeding me if you have no food?" Liam snapped. Patrick shrugged, "There's a burger joint down the street.."

"Which would work great if I wasn't currently being looked for by the cops." "He has a good point." Tyler interjected. "He can't leave here."

Patrick let out a heavy sigh, "Fiiiiiine." he dragged out. "I'll just go get him something then. What do you want, Liam?"

"I don't know."

"Fries? Pop? A burger? Seven burgers?" "Nothing... I'm not hungry."

"Then why the f-" Patrick growled and clenched his fists. "Why ask about food if you don't want anything to eat?"

Liam shrugged, "You interrupted my thoughts so it was my turn to annoy you." Tyler laughed, "You two are a messed up married couple."

Liam sat down on the chair again and crossed his arms. "By the looks of it he already is married to someone far worse than me." he said, smirking.

Patrick stayed leaning against the wall, his jaw clenching at his words but he just watched Liam for a moment. His pet was being annoying but the emotions running through him was making his soul seem far more delicious that it made his mouth water. He licked his lips and just thought about how close he was to getting that yummy soul. Sure he could easily take it now but having the soul get twisted in its emotions made it taste so much sweeter.

"So, since you aren't hungry, we can work on a plan to get those bullies and we have to do it tonight." Patrick said. He knew it was already a high risk being here and the longer they stayed, the higher the risk.

☽ CHAPTER TWENTY-FOUR ☾

Ash stood in a dark corner of the room just listening to the rain pounding against the cottage. He saw someone sleeping in bed but the boy quickly woke up hearing screams. Ash looked towards the door and waited to see who would come through. The boy on the bed had crawled off it but didn't move towards the door, instead of curled up behind a trunk. Ash had this dream before. He knew any moment now a dark figure was going to walk through the door and take away the boy. No, not a dark figure, a man. A man was going to save the boy. This dream felt so familiar to him but why? He knew this room.. He knew this house was located in the middle of the woods but he didn't understand this dream. He watched the door to the bedroom open slowly and watched the man walk into the room. He looked like someone he knew. The man spoke but Ash couldn't make out the words. He stood there watching as the man picked the boy up and turned towards the door to leave but not before Ash caught a glimpse of his eyes. They didn't look normal, they looked black but, then again the room was pretty dark, it was the orange that caught Ash's attention. Those eyes looked so black but for some weird reason they had bright orange pupils. What the hell?. Ash stepped forward but froze when he realized something else, that boy was him. This wasn't a dream, it was a memory that he couldn't fully remember.

He also realized that the man who came to save him as a boy was now the man he called father.

Ash jumped awake breathing heavily and looked around the room quickly. What was with these dreams? No, not dreams, it was a memory. Stavros didn't have those kinds of eyes though.

Ash grumbled, "You watch way too much TV" he murmured to himself. He glanced at the clock and saw it was just after six in the morning. He hardly remembered even going to bed. He knew they looked around the waterfall for Liam but found nothing and then they came home, ate, and Ash went up to his room. He sighed as he slipped out of bed and pulled on some clean sweats and a shirt. He ran his fingers through his hair as he headed to the bathroom and washed his face with some cold water.

Ash headed downstairs once he finished in the bathroom and wasn't surprised to see his dad sipping some coffee at the table while reading the paper.

"Morning." Ash murmured tiredly.

"Good morning." Stavros replied. "Do you want some breakfast?" Ash shook his head and got himself a glass of orange juice.

Stavros sighed softly, "They canceled school for today." he said. "Some kids from the school have turned up missing. Apparently they never made it home from school yesterday. Since they haven't been found and with the murders, the school board has decided to start winter break early."

Ash would have been happy about that if Liam wasn't missing. "I know some places have high crime rates but it's odd we are getting a lot of it."

Stavros nodded, "It is. This place is normally quiet but for some reason murders are happening every other day right now it seems.

Ash sat down and yawned softly while he checked his phone but wasn't surprised to see no new messages. "Are we looking for Liam today?" he asked.

"We had a pretty bad storm last night so I don't think we'll find Liam out on the streets but we can try. You need to eat something first though."

Ash nodded and stood up to get himself a bowl of cereal. He wasn't hungry enough to eat a whole lot right now.

"I heard you making some noises in your sleep. Did you have a nightmare?" Stavros asked. He had thought the nightmares had stopped by now.

"Yea." Ash said, not wanting to talk about how it was some kind of memory. He sat down at the table and began eating his cereal.

Stavros studied his son for a moment but didn't press the issue. He returned his attention to the paper and read it for a few more moments before he set it aside.

"Liam's mother was murdered this morning. The cops stopped by asking questions again but it doesn't seem like they are having any luck getting answers either." Stavros said.

Ash felt a cold chill run down his spine that caused him to shiver. He didn't like the woman but he knew if she was dead then the cops would be hunting for Liam even more. It seemed they already planned on pinning the blame on Liam unless they found something to prove it wasn't him.

Ash didn't speak about Liam's mother because he had nothing nice to say about it. Instead he looked at the paper and frowned as he yanked it closer to him. "Are these the guys who went missing?" he asked.

Stavros nodded, "You know them?"

"Not really…" "But?"

Ash sighed, "These are the four guys who bullied Liam in public school. They broke his nose once." he said, glancing up at his dad. "They only stopped because I beat their asses. They did try bullying him again at the start of highschool but I shut that down too."

Liam had told the principal but it never helped, the bullies would be suspended for a few days or spend time in detention but that was it and when they saw Liam again they always beat him worse for ratting them out.

Stavros frowned hearing Ash's words, though he was secretly proud of his son for sticking up to those bullies, and knew the cops would keep looking at Liam as a suspect if things didn't change quickly. Stavros knew this wasn't Liam, at least not fully, but he had no proof and everyone who made contact with Liam in the past was now turning up missing or dead. It wasn't looking good.

Ash cleaned up his bowl once he finished eating and checked his cell again. He had already tried calling Liam but, like always, he got no answer. It had only been a day or two since all this started with Liam but it had already been so draining, it felt like it's been weeks.

Ash headed to the front door and got his winter gear on to keep warm. He glanced back at his dad and waited for him to be ready before he opened the door and stepped outside. There were about seven inches of snow on the ground now and even though the sun was hidden by clouds, it wasn't horrible cold out.

"Where should we look first?" Stavros asked.

"We could check the mall to see if he'd go there to warm up?"

"No. Everyone knows who he is by now so he wouldn't go to the mall where he'd easily get caught."

Ash got into the car with a sigh as he tried thinking harder about where Liam would have gone. He came up blank. "I'm not sure where he'd go."

"Well we'll just keep driving around and keeping our eyes open." Stavros said. He pulled out of his driveway and drove down the street. Ash stared out the window watching everything they passed and hoping once again that they'd find Liam.

They drove around for hours and only stopped once to get some lunch before they went back to looking again. At times they'd stop to look down alleyways and even in some small stores but everywhere they went was a dead end. Ash didn't want to give up but he had no idea how much more of this he could even take. How did they know Liam was still alive? They checked in homeless shelters and under the bridge but no one had any information to share.

Stavros wanted to hunt down Patrick, he knew this shit was his doing, but he'd have to wait until Ash was sleeping so he didn't ask too many questions.

It was just before supper time and Stavros pulled up into their driveway. He turned off the car and looked over at Ash for a moment, then got out of the car and walked up to the front door. Ash waited a few moments but then joined his father inside.

He removed his winter gear and sat on the couch and stared at his phone.

☽ CHAPTER TWENTY-FIVE ☾

Patrick smirked as he watched Liam, the boy got that angry spark back into him. He seemed nervous at first, like Patrick would kill him for planning the murder of four boys, like he wasn't a demon that killed people all the time, but Patrick wouldn't harm his pet. Not yet, anyways. Tyler had grabbed those bullies yesterday on his walk and locked them up in a dumpster by the cliff, they were knocked out so they wouldn't be drawing attention.

Tyler was just wanting this to be over with, hating that they were going against orders and putting their asses on the line, just so Patrick could have Liam's soul. They had left the hotel early that morning to deal with Liam's mother. She had put up a good fight but something inside Liam snapped and he went absolutely crazy on her. After Liam had left a massive mess, they left her house and were currently in the woods. Liam was laughing like a lunatic, only pausing here and there to admire the blood all over his hands and clothing while also mumbling to himself. Tyler was listening for any unwanted guest and Patrick was staying close to Liam to whisper encouraging words.

"Come, little pet. It's time to get this over with." Patrick purred, enjoying his pet's mind snapping. Liam gave a nod and walked with Patrick towards the dumpster that held the bullies.

Patrick kicked the dumpster over with absolute ease, laughing darkly as the four boys went rolling out.

Tyler was enjoying this human who fought back against him. He had planned on just staying to the side and letting Patrick have all the fun but when they went rolling out, they jumped to their feet and were ready to fight, even if they were a bit unsteady on their feet. Tyler had grabbed one of them by the throat and squeezed pretty hard, the human had gasped for breath and even tried clawing Tyler's arm off. Tyler tore into that guy's throat with his fangs and sucked out his soul. Tyler normally liked taking his time with his feeding but he didn't see the point in drawing out a battle with these four worthless souls.

Patrick appeared in a thick yellow mist right in front of another bully, smirking darkly as he saw the fear in his eyes. Pat wanted to enjoy killing these useless humans but he was so close to his goal, he didn't want it dragging out. Pat moved fast, not even giving the boy time to move, and snapped his neck. He didn't want to ruin his taste buds with his disgusting soul or blood.

"Stop!" Ash shouted. He had stolen his fathers car and snuck out while he was in the shower. He knew it was stupid, being out here, but he knew his father was at the point of fully giving up and that was something Ash couldn't allow. He had arrived a few seconds ago, having seen Tyler ripping into someone's throat had frozen him to his spot. How did Tyler even do that? Wait, did he have fangs too?! Ash felt the breath leave him, a familiar panic starting to build up inside him. Ash flinched hearing bones breaking and looked over in time to see Patrick dropping a lifeless body. Ash felt bile rise in his throat and he had to look away so he didn't throw up.

"Kill him" Liam hissed at Tyler, pointing to a bully who was trying to escape, not even bothering to look at Ash.

Tyler grinned as he appeared in a white mist in front of another bully, who was trying to run, and shoved his claws into the male's stomach. He laughed as the human screamed, loving how he choked on the blood rising in his throat. Tyler ripped out the boy's insides, his white eyes glowing with enjoyment as the human dropped to the ground.

Ash stood frozen as he watched what was happening. Liam actually wanted this to happen? Liam looked thinner to Ash, paler too. He just looked so unhealthy and seeing him actually laugh as Tyler killed the bullies... it was sickening. His best friend was a sweet, caring guy. How could he allow this to happen? How could he want it to happen?

"Aren't my demon's just the sweetest?" Liam asked, laughing.

"Liam!" Ash called out, stumbling forward, his eyes wide with disbelief. Ash felt something stirring deep inside him, the hair on the back of his neck rose. They were seriously demons? How was that even possible?

'Nothing is truly what it seems' the pink- haired lady's words echoed in his head. Was this what she meant? Why didn't she just say "Hey, demons walk the earth." Not that Ash would have believed her, but still! And what about that man she was with? Just thinking about that man made a shiver run through him, was he a demon too? Was he involved with this?. That wouldn't make sense though, because now thinking of those words made Ash believe that maybe, just maybe, she was trying to help?

Liam glanced over at Ash and gave him a smirk but said nothing to him yet. It was clear he wasn't all there now and his eyes, that were once green, now were a dull yellow.

Tyler made quick work of the last bully because now that Ash was here, doing demon things was a risk. They couldn't kill this boy… or could they? Stavros wasn't around.

"Is it time to go?" Liam actually pouted at the thought. He was actually having fun with this. Patrick grinned, "Not yet, my pet. There is more fun to be had."

Liam was excited at those words until he remembered that Ash was there with them now. "What about him?" he asked, looking at Ash as though he was a stranger.

Patrick glanced at Ash and shrugged, "What do you want to do with him?" he asked.

Liam tapped his chin as he thought about that question. What should he do with him? He was getting in the way and ruining his fun time but he didn't have a chance to answer because Ash spoke again.

"You can't do this, Liam. You have to let this go and just come with me now, please?" he begged.

Liam growled, "I can do this! I got two demons with me and they'll make sure this happens. They'll set everything right for me."

Ash was shocked, "What happened to you?" he whispered, his body trembling as a mixture of emotions ran through him.

Liam didn't answer that, he didn't want to waste time talking about this shit. He just wanted to see more people die, to hear their screams and see their pretty blood on the ground.

"Liam, please come to my house. We can fix this." Ash pleaded. He had no idea how the hell they'd fix this but he had to try something, right? His father could sort all this out somehow and keep Liam safe. He would do that, wouldn't he?

Liam laughed darkly as he stared at Ash, "It's best you don't get in my way, Ashton. I don't want to hurt you but if you try stopping me then you'd give me no choice," he growled.

How did this even happen? Ash couldn't believe what was happening and he wished he just stayed at home so he didn't have to witness any of this.

☽ CHAPTER TWENTY-SIX ☾

"Liam!" Ash snapped, "You have to stop this! You can't use them to kill everyone who has wronged you!" Ash's voice rose. He felt like running over to him and beating some sense into him or just grabbing him and dragging him home. Ash was still trying to figure out what was even going on! Demons? What? Liam had demons working for him? How the hell did that even happen? How does that even work?

Liam smirked "You don't seem to understand that I, in fact, can. With these two helping me I can do anything! I can hurt those assholes who hurt me!" He laughed bitterly.

"Liam.. Please... Don't do this," Ash pleaded. What was happening? How did his best friend become so... So dark? So messed up like this? "You don't have to be like them.. Things will get better." He tried to reason. Ash was willing to try anything, he needed his best friend to just snap out of this blood lust.

"I disposed of my father and mother." Liam purred. "Now it's time to get rid of the rest of those shit heads that ever thought it was funny to beat me." Liam nearly yelled out. "I'LL SHOW ALL OF THEM!" He screamed.

"Liam STOP!" Ash felt tears streaming down his face. He saw the look in his best friend's eyes, that blood lust, the love of having so much power, so much control, he lost his best friend. The boy he was looking up at was only a stranger to him now. His body was screaming at him to move, to run back home to safety, but he couldn't. He couldn't leave Liam alone with these two assholes.

"I said get the hell out of my way." Liam snapped. "Remove him!" He snarled, turning his attention to Tyler who stood on his left. Tyler had an evil grin on his face, the air around him swirled around like a tornado was surrounding him. Tyler's shirt was already stained with blood and shredded along the sleeves from someone who had fought back against him. Blood dripped from his mouth and fingertips and his eyes were pure white and Ash could tell that Tyler was enjoying himself, he was amused and all too happy to cause chaos and suffering to someone.

Patrick hadn't said a word this whole time, nor did he move from Liam's side, but Ash realized that Patrick had been speaking, he was whispering whatever bullshit words into Liam's ear.

Patrick was still clean, he wasn't covered in blood like Tyler, his black shirt and pants were still nicely kept but the look on his face, it scared Ash. Patrick looked at Liam like he was a meal, like a starving person would look at a steak and it unnerved him.

Ash looked back at Tyler, catching movement from the corner of his eye, then suddenly, Tyler was right in front of him. He moved with such speed that he had just been a blur. Ash wasn't sure if he had super speed or if he simply just appeared in front of Ash.

Ash stepped back but Tyler quickly grabbed the front of his shirt and yanked him close. He could smell the foul blood on Tyler's breath, could hear the deep chuckle leaving the demon's throat. "I'm going to enjoy this, pathetic boy" The demon hissed. Ash could have sworn that the demon's voice was an echo, it didn't sound like a normal voice anymore. It sounded far away but the words repeated in his mind over and over again.

Ash grabbed at Tyler's arm, his eyes wide with fear and a scream catching in his throat. He struggled, hard, trying to free himself from the demon's grasp but it wasn't working. He tried punching the man, slamming his fist against his chest, even tried kicking him but he was panicking. He couldn't remember the defensive moves his father taught him, couldn't remember how to breathe, to scream. The demon was unfazed by Ash's attempts and, honestly, Ash was starting to tire out.

Everything in him screamed to keep fighting but what was the use now? He couldn't win against a demon and no one knew he was here.

"Might as well give up, you can't win," Tyler laughed darkly. He raised a hand, Ash's eyes focusing on his long claws, he went to shout but was cut off feeling a harsh pain on his face. Ash screamed as pain erupted on his face, the blood filling all his senses. He had to close his left eye because blood kept burning and blinding him. Ash let out a sob, not just from the excruciating pain, but knowing his best friend allowed this to happen, knowing his best friend commanded this to happen.

Ash opened his mouth, ready to lash out at Tyler, but then suddenly something grabbed the back of his shirt and ripped him away from Tyler. At first, Ash thought it was Patrick wanting a turn, but when he was finally released and able to collect himself, he realized it was his father standing there right in front of Tyler.

"You foolish piece of filth," Stavros growled at Tyler. He was pissed and about to unleash years of pent up rage on him. "You had your fun and decided to ruin it by attacking my son?" He snarled out. He was beyond pissed. Ash felt the air get cold, to the point of freezing, and it was silent. Dead silent. No wind, bugs, birds, nothing. Ash wiped at his eyes, trying to clear them of blood and tears so everything wasn't blurry. Ash collapsed on the ground when a sudden, overwhelming, feeling of dread washed over him. He was trembling but couldn't tell if it was because it was freezing out, or because he was fighting against the urge to just lay down and slip away into nothing.

Stavros didn't give Tyler a chance to say anything or even move, as his clawed hand slammed right into Tyler's chest. "You are done bringing terror to this world." Stavros smirked, reaching his hand in further to grab Tyler's spine.

Ash struggled to focus, the fight in him slipping away quickly, but then he heard a scream in his head. *Wake up!* it was the same one from that dream he had, why would he be hearing that right now? He had no time to dwell on that because his body suddenly awoke with life again.

Ash sat up, looking over to his father and seeing something shine in his hand. He was able to focus just as his father sliced all the way through Tyler's neck with a short sword. Ash shut his eyes tightly, wishing he hadn't seen that and not wanting to see anymore, he heard the gurgling sound of Tyler choking on his own blood. He heard what sounded like Tyler trying to speak, but he had no idea what he was trying to say.

Stavros jerked back, his grip on Tyler's spine tightening as he pulled his hand, and spine, from his body and chuckled darkly as the body fell to the ground. Stavros glanced back at Ash but his focus didn't last long on him because Patrick let out a roar of rage.

"You son of a bitch!" Liam snapped. "Why would you do that? HOW did you do that?!" He hadn't thought something like that would happen.

"You ordered your demon to attack my son, I wouldn't just sit back and allow that to happen." Stavros replied calmly, flicking the blade to the side to whisk away the blood. He knew he couldn't reach Liam, the boy's mind was already too far gone. Patrick had done his work well and twisted the boy's mind bad enough that the boy was even willing to attack his own best friend. "Very easily." He smirked in response to his second question.

Patrick lunged at Stavros but he was not as big or strong as him so he was easily grabbed by the throat and pinned against a tree. "You really want to die like him?" Stavros growled out. "You killed my brother, I'll kill you," Patrick snapped.

Stavros laughed and then let out a growl when Patrick shot his knee up quickly and it impacted with Starovs' lower stomach. He released his hold on Patrick and jumped back a few feet, Ash was just watching this all happening, trying to wrap his mind around what was going on. They moved so fast and Ash couldn't keep up, especially when the fear of losing his father crept into his mind.

"Dad watch out!" Ash yelled out. Patrick ran straight at Stavros but he didn't have a weapon, he just had long claws that were ready to rip into him. Ash took a step forward but then stopped himself and looked up at Liam, maybe he could convince Liam to stop this? Ash watched his father for a moment with his good eye and then pulled off his shirt. It was still freezing out so being shirtless wasn't the smartest idea but he had to ignore the cold right now and get to Liam. He pressed the shirt against the claw marks on his face and removed his belt, wrapping it around his head to keep his eye covered, and ran towards Liam. He didn't know how Liam turned out this way but he had to try and fix this. Fix him. He paused, only for a second, hearing his father let out a grunt but Ash quickly returned his attention to Liam, he knew his father would be fine. Ash needed his best friend back and he was determined to make it happen.

☽ CHAPTER TWENTY-SEVEN ☾

"You honestly think you can kill me?" Stavros laughed as he jumped back from Patrick. He had slash marks across his chest, the blood soaking through the black shirt that was shredded enough that it seemed like it was about to just fall off anyways. Patrick was in worse shape, he had cut marks on his neck, shoulders, and a few on his arms.

"I can try," Patrick hissed out. "You aren't all powerful, there's a way to kill you and I'll figure it out." He smirked.

"Sometime before you die in this fight?" Stavros chuckled bitterly. "How foolish can you seriously be?" He growled as he lunged forward. He slashed at Patrick but he was quick to roll out of the way and stabbed his claws into Stavros' side, just under the rib cage, and earned a snarl of pain from Stavros and a backhand across the face to get knocked away.

Patrick grunted from the hit but rolled to his feet, staying crouched down, ready to attack once again.

"You should have left when I gave that order. Your brother would still be alive if you two knew how to fucking listen." Stavros growled, narrowing his glowing orange eyes. "What's worse is you fools attacked my son, did you really think I'd let that slide?" Stavros hissed.

"No," Patrick grinned. "He isn't even your son though, why care about this boy who has nothing to offer you?" He questioned.

Stavros threw his long knife, smirking when it slammed into Patrick's shoulder and he let out a cry of pain. "He has much to offer me but that is no business of yours seeing as you'll be dead soon anyway."

"We'll see." Patrick snapped, ripping the knife out and throwing it at Stavros.

"Liam!" Ash panted out, finally reaching him "Please, stop this!" He felt like he was about to pass out, probably from the blood loss. He quickly walked towards Liam, unable to run currently, and fell to his knees once he reached him. "You can stop this, please!" Ash pleaded with him again. Liam spun to face him, having been so focused on the fight he didn't notice that Ash had approached him, and narrowed his eyes. "Stop it? Why? What does stopping it do for me?" He spat.

"What does killing my father do for you? What does harming your best friend do? You got rid of your father, why keep doing this?" Ash snapped back, gesturing to his face. "Do you seriously need to keep killing people just because you have a demon?" Ash questioned. "Please.. Liam, don't let him kill my father.. I can't lose him," he whispered.

Liam watched Ash for a moment before he shook his head. "I can't stop.. I don't know how. They tormented me! They all did!" he shouted. "My father, my mother, they should have been killed a long time ago and those bullies? They shouldn't be allowed to live and make others suffer!" He growled out. He narrowed his eyes once more and looked over at Stavros and Patrick. He watched the fighting, watched as Patrick would land a blow but Stavros remained standing and always seemed to land a harder blow.

"Someone will win this fight." Liam smirked.

Ash felt his eye water again and he removed the belt wrapped around his head and the shirt "Liam." he whispered, looking up at him from his spot on his knees. "No one will win this fight," he whispered. He had five long gashes on the left side of his face, starting just below his hair line and ending just above his jaw going straight down; they barely missed Ash's left eye.Liam looked at Ash once again and blinked seeing the gashes on his face. He felt his heart break at the sight, he made that happen, he let that happen.. To his best friend. Who did such a thing to their best friend? "I... " he looked away, ashamed. He felt confused, he was trying to work out what he should do. Did he want to stop this? He knew how much pain Ash would be in if he lost his father.. "Patrick.." he said softly, he knew the demon would hear him easily enough. "Stop. Don't kill him" he whispered. He looked at Ash again with tears running down his face, "I'm so sorry.. I.. I don't know what came over me" he whispered.

Patrick was at Liam's side in an instant "What have you done?" he hissed at Ash. "You've ruined what I was creating.. Now he's broken" he growled out. He was panting, the wounds were taking its toll on him but Patrick would need more than a few slashes or stab wounds to die. Stavros had a special blade that was made from demon bones covered in titanium for strength. It was one way to kill any demon but they all had their own main weakness, the trick was trying to find it.

"I didn't ruin him.. I fixed him from what you were doing to him" Ash snapped.

"You had your fun, now leave." Stavros, who was now standing behind Ash, hissed out. "Liam is no longer yours to control." he narrowed his eyes.

Patrick laughed darkly, standing way too close to Liam for Ash's comfort, "True.. I had my fun and now it's over." he hissed. He smirked darkly and quickly spun on Liam, shoving his hand into Liam's chest and crushing his heart slowly, his body began to heal as it devoured Liam's soul through his fingertips.

"NO! YOU SON OF A BITCH!" Ash screamed. He jumped to his feet but Stavros was quick to wrap both arms around Ash and pull him back to keep him away from the demon. Ash felt something inside him snap and all he wanted to do was kill Patrick and bathe in his pathetic blood.

"Ash, there's nothing you can do!" he said loudly over Ashs' screaming and crying. "NO! LET ME GO! Liam! Liam, LOOK AT ME!" Ash sobbed out.

Patrick laughed darkly and pulled his hand out of Liam's chest and smirked as the boy's body dropped to the ground, crimson blood bleeding into the snow.

Ash looked at his friend's lifeless body and everything around him blurred. He knew Patrick said something but honestly all he could do was scream, sob, and stare at his best friend's body. He tried yanking away from his father but he held onto him firmly.

His father finally released him when Patrick vanished like smoke into a breeze. Ash stumbled over to Liam's body and sobbed as he dropped to his knees and pulled Liam's head onto his lap and held him tightly. He kept apologizing, wishing he had helped him better, wishing he did things differently, begging him to return but nothing worked. He sat there, cradling his best friend's head, sobbing. Everything around him was like white noise, he couldn't focus on anything, he heard his father murmur something but he had no idea what on earth he said however, moments later, Ash was being pulled away from his friend's body. He struggled, trying to stay with Liam, not ready to let him go or admit he was gone. His father was strong but gentle as he pulled him up from Liam's body, wrapping his arms around him and cradling his head as the boy sobbed into his chest.

Stavros felt the pain coming from his son and hated himself for it, knowing he could have stopped this sooner, but it wasn't his place. He knew nothing he said or did would make this better, so he just held Ash tight and let him cry.

Ash had no idea when his father called the police, but they were here and already pestering for answers. Ash planned on ignoring them, not knowing how to even begin to explain what happened, but luckily, his father talked to them.

"We need to back up," Stavros murmured. He pulled back from Ash for just a moment, taking off his coat and wrapping it around his son feeling how frozen he was. When Ash didn't move, Stavros scooped him up and held him close, taking a few steps away from Liam's body.

The police tried speaking to Ash again, needing his statement, but he didn't say a word, he couldn't. How could he put what happened into words? They eventually released him because Stavros gave his own statement on what had happened, but they would need Ash to give his statement soon.

Ash felt so numb by the end of it all, he couldn't cry anymore, couldn't think. He hardly noticed them taking Liam's body, hardly noticed being brought to the car and driven home. He barely even noticed Stavros speaking to him. Everything in the world was just faded, far away, just out of his reach but he couldn't care about that right now, the image of Liam's death replayed in his mind over and over again.

The next few days were such a blur, Liam's family gathered, they did the memorial, Ash didn't speak at all then either. He hadn't spoken since they took Liam's body away from him. The day of the funeral was a blur as well, he remembered people saying words and Ash had tried writing something down to say but he couldn't find his voice. This wasn't real, it couldn't be real, it was a huge nightmare and he needed to wake up but for some reason he couldn't. Ash had nightmares of that day, had cried many times, and was still having a hard time believing it was even real.

Ash was the last one standing by Liam's grave. He stared down at the coffin, he knew his father was beside him but also trying to give him space. For the first time since that day Ash had started to think about everything else that had happened. He watched how his father fought against Tyler, how he killed him like it was nothing and even though Ash knew his father got injured fighting Patrick, he had no wounds. Ash's claw marks down his face had gotten stitches and still healing, though the doctor couldn't believe a cougar did it. It's what Stavros had to say because saying a human did it was unbelievable but a wild cat attack was the closest thing the scratch marks looked like it could be from, it couldn't be some human who did it. Human? No.

Patrick and Tyler were not human. His father was not human.

Ash stared down at the coffin and, for the first time since his best friend was killed, spoke to his father without looking at him. "What are you?" he whispered. His voice was hoarse from lack of use and from crying so much the last few days.

He heard his father sigh and take a few steps forward but then stopped, not wanting to get too close just yet. There was silence and Ash was starting to think that he wouldn't get an answer but when his father spoke, he said one word and it made Ash turn to stare at him in horror. "Demon."

☽ EPILOGUE ☾

"I warned you all this was going to happen," a deep, angry, male voice growled out. The man sat in a dark room with four others. His straight shoulder-length black hair contrasted with the dark red tips and his three-day old stubble that was sported on his chin. It was hard to judge his height with him sitting down but if one would take a guess, he stood well over six foot five, maybe even six foot seven. His lack of shirt shown let his tan muscular body peek out from the black leather trench coat he wore with matching black jeans and steel toe shoes. The room was dark with only a few candles casting dim light around it, letting the large table that could fit twenty eastly show its beautiful red hew. Two servants poured red liquid into cups with ease for those sitting around the table.

With a click of her tongue a woman spoke "Calm down, Killian." She rolled her ice blue eyes as she looked lazily within her cup. "We all knew this was going to happen, but the question is now, what are we going to do about it?" Her tone made it very clear she thought herself above everyone here and if the flip of her long blonde wavy hair didn't give it away her face should as it watched them with little to no amusement. Rogue was better known for her looks then her personality, having a body that most women paid top dollar for. Her luscious curves were hugged tightly in her blue dress that contrasted beautifully with her pale flawless skin. Shifting her weight, she moved to a chair that she could barely see over, even with her heels she only stood five eight.

"This is why we are here, Rogue" another male's voice spoke up in a matter-of-fact way. "We need to figure this stuff out." The man paced the room slowly, holding his cup in his dark colored hand. "Lucian and Dakota couldn't make it here, but they always seem to side with Stavros anyways" He informed the group as he walked into the little candlelight the room offered, showing off his deep rich umber skin and chestnut eyes, his blood red shirt and blue jeans only adding to his look. He sighed as he ran his hand through his curly brown hair showing off his large, muscled build "Anyway, we can't kill him, nor do our powers fully affect him either" he muttered the last part into his cup as he took a sip. It was irritating but it was how things worked for them. It wasn't like they couldn't fight each other or use their powers on the others of the Eight but you had to know the others weakness. A weakness that they never revealed.

Rogue rolled her eyes. "At one point we all sided with him but this is going over the line." "How?" Killian rose a brow slowly. "Tyler and Patrick acted without permission from Stavros. He had a right to fight against them."

Jaded narrowed his eyes slowly. "If that is how you feel then why are you bitching about this?" "Who said that was the issue I had?" Killian hissed.

"Alright. Fine. What *is* your issue then?" Rogue asked.

"What issue do I ever have with anyone?" Killian growled lowly. "He has that stupid little rodent living with him. It's disgusting. How can anyone be willing to put up with gross little things?" He shuddered. "It's foul and shouldn't be allowed. Even livestock shouldn't be allowed to have those disgusting horrible shits but since they are our food, I allow it."

"Wait" Shadow interrupted with a look of entertainment plastered across his face. His bright red eyes scrunched from his grin as he watched the four through his black bone straight hair, in a brighter place you would see the silver and gray highlights within it "You, Killian, are here not because of Stavros, like these three idiots." his long claw-like red nails pointed to the other three within the room before landing back onto Killian "But because he has a child?" he couldn't help but laugh as he sat up straighter in his chair giving away his large height. He could well be seven foot tall, maybe an inch short.

"Shut your mouth, Shadow," Killian barked out. "Children are horrible little things that really shouldn't be around at all."

Shadow lend forward in his chair letting the candle light up his face showing off the red dragon tattoo that circled his right eye as its tail ended beside his lips that showed a fanged grin "You know I would pay to see you actually raise one of those 'disgusting horrible shits' as you call them" he sits back in his chair "It would be highly amusing, I swear people would pay millions just to watch you with that child for an hour" he laughed.

Killian gagged. "I'd never have one! And I've had sex many times." His voice was a snarl. "Two times does not count as 'many,'" Rogue said with a soft giggle.

Killian shot to his feet and glared at her. "Now both of you shut up!" He snapped. "My sex life isn't what we are here to talk about."

"Or lack thereof..." Jaded muttered. Shadow almost dropped his drink from how hard he laughed at Killian's face.

Killian hissed at Jaded and went to lunge at him but Shadow moved fast and pinned the angry demon Lord against the wall with his shadows. "There is no fighting here, Killian," Shadow pointed out.

"I'm surprised you were willing to actually touch him to stop him." Jaded said. He and Shadow never got along all that great.

"Well it's not like I'm going to get any sexual diseases from him," Shadow said with a smirk. He moved away from Killian just as the man swung to punch him. Shadow tsked. "Now now, behave child or I'll have to give you a spanking."

Killian growled deep in his throat. "I hate all of you."

Shadow just gave a laugh. "Can you name anyone you *don't* hate?" He asked, waiting a brief moment. "Exactly," he added, when Killian just looked away and said nothing.

The sound of a fist hitting the wooden table made the room come to a stop in its bickering. All eyes turned to a warm skinned woman covered in scars from head to toe. Her dark green eyes looked over their faces before shaking her head making her long curly ash colored hair bounce "All of you shut up" she signed her face matching what she signed with her hands "Actually think about what we are going to do!" Tabitha could speak but her speech honestly was forgotten by those around her for she hasn't spoken in years, she rolled her tongue in her mouth in discomfort from the burn she had gotten in her mouth when she was younger. "We can't kill Stavros" She placed her hands in her lap running her fingers over the blue denim that seemed a bright blue thanks to her white tank top.

Jaded groaned. "We know that" he sighed heavily as he rubbed his temples, glaring up at the four of them "So, any great ideas?"

Shadow shrugged slightly. "I honestly don't care. You four can come up with some stupid plan but leave me out of whatever it is because I already know you guys will mess it all up." They were idiots when it came to planning anything together because all they ever did was fight, and when the time actually came to do what they planned they always refused to work together and decided to do things on their own terms.

"Then why are you even here?" Killian asked. "You already knew what we'd be talking about so why waste our time having to listen to your useless words?" he growled.

Shadow smiled. "Oh baby, you know I could never stay away from you for too long." He winked which succeeded in pissing Killian off. "Beside the obvious, it's my fucking house."

"You are disgusting," Killian snarled. His face was a mask of disgust as he glared at Shadow. "You keep talking like that and I'll kick all these losers out just so I can really show you how much I've missed you," Shadow purred. He licked his lips and looked Killian over slowly. "I'm so glad you decided to come here shirtless. Maybe next time I'll be really lucky and you'll end up forgetting your pants, or, better yet, you'll arrive naked." Shadow shivered with joy at the thought.

Killian felt like he was going to throw up. "Sorry, disgusting filth, you aren't my type." Shadow snorted. "I didn't think you had a type, since you don't have sex."

"If we weren't in your domain I would be ripping you to shreds!" Killian snarled. Shadow gave a slow grin.

"Are sure you don't mean you'd shred my clothes?"

"Enough!" Rogue snapped. "We are getting nowhere with you two going on like this. Focus!" She crossed her arms over her chest.

Shadow rolled his eyes "Someone likes to ruin my fun" Sucking air through his pursed lips he pointed his finger around him within a lazy motion "Next time go to someone else's place okay?" seeing no one paying him mind he crossed his arms "whatever, keeping talking then"

He wasn't really shocked to see them wanting to gather within his home, he had built his home with his power over the shadows. It made sure that not only did nothing come in but nothing got out if he willed it. Which made his power something that could work on all of them to an extent and right now pushing them outside was seeming better by the moment

Tabitha hit the table again. "You fool. If you have nothing to say that would be helpful, sit down and shut up." Her eyes glaring at Killian before turning her eyes to the group "This is going in circles. We are getting nowhere in this." Killian slowly sinks back into his seat.

Jaded mumbled to himself about being stuck with useless children. He cleared his throat and spoke. "We are here to discuss Stavros. He has grown soft over the years because of that boy he has. How can he call himself a demon Lord if he can't even act like one? He acts like a human and we can't allow that."

"Is it really that bad?" Shadow asked with a sigh. "The boy will die at some point and Stavros will return to himself when that happens. Humans only live for a handful of years, that's nothing compared to the millions of centuries that we live."

"None of us are that old," Killian snorted in false confidence. "And even if the gross thing does die, Stavros is attached to it now and it's not like he'll go back to how he used to be when it does. We can't sit around and wait for that to happen."

"Exactly." Rogue chimed in. "It needs to be handled soon or else it'll mess everything up." "Everything?" Shadow asked. He raised a brow slowly as he looked at her. "What do we have planned exactly? Because last time I checked we are demons with very simple minds. All we seem to care about is our next meal, fun sexy times, ruling over other demons and fucking shit up. None of that involves actually planning anything and if you do have to plan it then you are just a terrible demon who really shouldn't be lord of anything." His voice was a soft growl as he spoke.

Rogue glared at Shadow and flipped him off. "That may be your plan but the rest of us would like to do a lot more with our lives."

"You mean our never ending life?" Shadow asked. "We've been alive for a really long time and have only planned the wars, which didn't take much planning. Humans are greedy little assholes and are so simple to control or push into destroying each other. We are demons they don't even know about, and they sure as hell don't know we pull all their strings. Humans are needy, greedy, cowardly, little pests. Really, the list could go on and on about what they are and, sadly, with how you guys are freaking out about this shit, it just makes you sound like whiny little humans." He liked demons as much as he liked humans and he couldn't stand humans. He didn't need souls like the rest of them, even though he did feed on them when he was bored.

Rogue growled low in her throat but before she could say anything Jaded spoke.

"Both of you knock it off. Yes, Shadow, we all know how you feel about all this, and at times I do agree that some of us sound like whiny humans, but this is a serious matter so at least act like it. Like damn, I know we can't stand to be around each other but at least act grown up long enough for us to finish this conversation so we can just leave." His voice was stern, and he'd hit them all over the head if he could, but he knew that it would just start another fight and he really just wanted to get this over with so he could leave.

Shadow grumbled some curses to himself but said nothing more as he sat in his chair and played around with his cup.

Killian sighed heavily. "As it has been pointed out, we can't kill Stavros." He glanced around at them. "We do not know his normal weaknesses but he does have one that he hadn't planned on having," he said.

Rogue tilted her head curiously. "Oh? And what exactly is that?"

Tabitha shook her head slowly. "*I know where you are going with this, Killian, and it isn't a good idea.*" She signed.

"Why not?" Killian asked. "You guys wanted to solve this problem and we have a way to do it."

"*No,*" Tabitha signed. "*You have a way for him to want war against all of us.*"

Killian gave a small smirk. "You are talking to the Lord of war, dumbass. I'd be more than happy to start one with him." He always did enjoy a good war, especially against a powerful opponent. He liked when his wars went on for years and he knew Rogue loved it since she was the Lord of destruction.

"What is it?" Rogue barked out. She hated when they did this. Why couldn't they share the full plan first and then argue about whether it was a good idea or not?

Killian smirked again as he sat back in his chair and looked at them all. "Ash," he growled. "He raised that boy for ten years and has grown attached to it. It has made Stavros soft which isn't good for us. We need to remove Ash so Stavros can return to us."

Shadow snorted but remained silent. He knew it was a stupid idea and he wasn't about to have a part in it.

"You'd never get Dakota or Lucian to agree," Jaded pointed out. "Or Shadow." Shadow spoke for himself.

"Or Shadow," Jaded added, rolling his eyes. "If you are going to try getting that boy away from Stavros we all need to work together."

"No, we don't." Killian said. He sighed and shook his head slowly. "The pest goes to school and he does leave Stavros' sight so we can do it when he's alone." He gave a shrug.

"What are we suppose to do with him?" Rogue asked. "It's not like we can just lock him up somewhere and hope Stavros never finds him again. Stavros will tear the world apart to find him." She sighed. This was giving her a headache and she really wished she had blown this meeting off.

Killian growled as he slowly stood. "Are you completely brain dead? Like honestly, do you know how to think? Or even follow a conversation?"

"It's not my fault you don't give all the information right away," Rogue snapped at him. "Please, oh great know-it-all, what is the plan? Where would you keep him? What would we do with him?"

Tabitha rolled her eyes and watched as Jaded continued to pace. They were idiots and how she had managed to stay here without trying to rip someone's throat out was amazing.

Killian ran his fingers through his hair and took a sip of his drink. He licked his lips and gave Rogue a hard look. "To put things into simple words for you, simple minded female, we wouldn't keep it anywhere."

"Than where-"

"We will kill him." Killian cut her off. He smirked and slowly wiped the blood from his bottom lip with his thumb. "We will punish Stavros by killing Ash."